A DOORWAY OF MIRRORS

By
Katrina Mandrake-Johnston

Cover and illustrations by
Katrina Mandrake-Johnston

Order this book online at www.trafford.com
or email orders@trafford.com

Most Trafford titles are also available at major online book retailers.

Print information available on the last page.

ISBN: 978-1-4120-6255-8 (sc)

Trafford rev. 05/20/2019

 www.trafford.com

North America & international
toll-free: 1 888 232 4444 (USA & Canada)
fax: 812 355 4082

< A Doorway Of Mirrors >   < By Katrina Mandrake-Johnston >   < 1 >

CHAPTER 1

When Billy came downstairs that morning, he was delighted to hear the crackling sizzle of bacon frying. His mom was standing at the stove in her pink housecoat and fuzzy slippers. She yawned and wiggled the bacon strips around in the pan with her spatula.

"Morning Mum," Billy said as he sat down at the table and poured himself a tall glass of frosty orange juice. He always loved to get that first glass, just after his mom had made up the pitcher. There were always little crystals of ice that hadn't quite melted yet and Billy thought this to be just the right thing to make it extra delicious. Of course his younger sister always had to argue that it didn't matter because it was all the same juice and whether the ice crystals were there or not didn't change the taste.

"I'm making the big breakfast your sister asked for. Eggs, bacon, and the whole works," his mom told him before letting out another huge yawn, "I didn't get up early enough to make the pancakes. There wasn't enough time to fry the batter. She'll have to be happy with toast. We'll have to rush through our breakfast as it is."

His mom popped a couple pieces of bread into the toaster and then dished out the bacon beside each mound of scrambled eggs on each of the three plates. Billy scooped a forkful of eggs off his sister's plate onto his… and received an annoyed look from his mother.

Billy tried to justify it by saying, "She had a bit more, Mum. I was just making it so it's even, is all."

"Sure you were," she said with a sly smile, "Isn't Jenny up yet? She made such a fuss last night about wanting to get there early, and needing a big breakfast, and all that. She better not be in bed still."

"Dad get off to work okay?" Billy asked taking a bite of the crisp and crunchy bacon, "He looked so tired last night and his cold seemed to be getting worse."

"He keeps insisting that it's allergies and you know how stubborn he can be about getting extra rest," she told him, "You better run up there and make sure she's up. She's been so excited and nervous about the junior chess competition these past few weeks. She'll kill us if we let her sleep in. I've got to take out the garbage before I forget."

"Okay Mum," he said as he hurried up the stairs.

"Tell her that her food's getting cold. That'll get her up," his mom called after him.

Billy knocked on her bedroom door. "Hey Jenny! Mum says it's time to get up!" he called out.

He was about to head back downstairs again, but something stopped him. He wasn't sure what it was. It was like a cold chill ran down over his body. Something felt wrong.

He knocked again on the door, this time louder. "Jenny? You in there? Breakfast is ready. You better hurry up or you're going to be late."

There was no answer. Usually, she would yell at him to stop bugging her. She would say that she'd be down when she was good and ready and to stop rushing her all the time. She would at least say something; she would never ignore him completely like this. "Jenny?" he called again, but he still had that weird feeling that something wasn't quite right.

He turned the knob and opened the door. She always yelled at him for coming into her room. "Jenny? Are you in here?" he asked into the room from the doorway. He glanced over to the bathroom door at the end of the hall. She wasn't in there.

Billy was worried now. He thought to himself, "*Maybe she caught Dad's cold. Maybe that's why she's not answering. She's probably so sick, she's not waking up. I've been sick like that before, where you end up sleeping all day*." Another chill ran down his body.

< A Doorway Of Mirrors >   < By Katrina Mandrake-Johnston >   < 2 >

He stepped into her room and turned on the light. His eyes fell on dolls and other stuffed animals, unicorn ornaments, and her many books. However, her bed was empty, and she was not in her room.

The huge grandfather clock was in the corner, its pendulum swinging back and forth. It was so out of place, but she had insisted on keeping it. Sometimes, Billy thought his parents would let her do anything she wanted. It seemed that way so many times. The clock had been their grandfather's, and he had recently passed away. It would have been put on the list of things to sell in the garage sale their mother was planning, but Jenny had pleaded with her that if the only reason they were getting rid of the clock was because they had no room to keep it, that she would have it in her room. She promised that she would take perfect care of it and that the chimes wouldn't keep her awake at all.

After a few nights, Jenny had confided in him that the clock was driving her crazy. She wasn't going to admit this to their parents of course. Jenny had realized that they were trying to teach her a lesson by allowing her to keep the clock, but she loved that clock and she wasn't going to let it go.

Jenny was very smart for her age, and Billy was sure she would win the junior chess competition. But she wouldn't even be able to enter if she arrived at the school even a few minutes late. She had stressed that importance so many times last night. Where could she possibly be?

Billy ran down the stairs and shouted, "Mum! Mum! Jenny's gone!"

"What's that honey?" his mom asked drying the soapy dishwater off her hands.

"Jenny! She's not in her room. She's gone!" he said frantically.

His mom gave him a confused look, her eyebrows squishing together with worry, "Well did you check the bathroom?"

"Of course I…" Billy began to say, and then he heard Jenny's voice behind him.

"Hello, Mum. Hello, Billy," said Jenny, "I was just in my room getting dressed."

"Billy, that was not funny at all. Don't you ever play a trick like that again," his mother scolded, "You had me worried sick there for a minute. I wouldn't have known what to think. Just to imagine… Oh, don't you ever do something like that again. You hear me? It's the look on your face that did it. I really believed you! Do you remember what your father and I spoke to you about on how important trust is within a family?"

"Yes, Mum, but…" he started to say.

"Just finish your breakfast," she told him, "I have to be up to your grandfather's house to sort through more of his things after I drop you two off at the school."

"Why are we having this for breakfast?" Jenny whispered to Billy.

"It's bacon and eggs. Remember? You asked Mum to make it 'cause of the big competition today," he explained. As he looked at his sister, he noticed that there was something odd about her. He couldn't tell exactly what, but her eyes, it was almost as if they lacked a certain life to them. She was probably just tired.

"Oh, I'm not in my right mind today! I forgot to call Aunt Bethany. I need her to pick you up from school! Oh, how could I have forgotten!" their mother said grabbing the phone and quickly punching in the numbers.

After a few moments, she sighed a breath of relief, "Oh, I'm so glad I caught you. I have to sort through some things at my dad's place. Could you watch the kids today? I should really spend all day there or I won't get anything done. You know how it is, so many memories. It's hard to get rid of anything really," she paused, listening anxiously to the reply.

"And you'll be able to pick them up from school?" she asked, waving at the children for

< A Doorway Of Mirrors >   < By Katrina Mandrake-Johnston >   < 3 >

them to quickly finish up their food. "Oh, that's great then. Thank-you so much... Okay, I'll phone you later then to check in... Alright... Bye."

She hung up the phone saying, "Okay, everything's taken care of then. She'll be watching you this afternoon and probably do the same for the next few days. I've got to get ready or we'll never be to the school on time. You know which door we're supposed to go in, right Jenny?"

A strange look came over Jenny's face, as if she were trying far too hard to come up with an answer, and then she said, "Yes," but by this time their mother had already left the room.

"Are you feeling okay?" Billy asked, "Where were you really? I went to check on you, and you weren't in your room."

"I am fine," she answered plainly, "I was in my room getting dressed."

Billy didn't know what to say; he didn't want to argue with her.

"This is an interesting piece," Jenny said picking up the chess piece from the table, "Is it a unicorn? I like unicorns."

Billy had an awful feeling inside and said, "Jenny, that's your lucky knight. You had it since you were three. Remember? The white knight?"

"Yes, this is my lucky knight I had since I was three," Jenny stated, "But I am just wondering why is it only a horse? Did the little knight get broken off? Is there some sort of use for this that I should be aware of?"

"Who are you?!" he asked confused and a little afraid. This was not his sister, and the more he stared at her, the more he saw it. This person looked like Jenny, but it was not her.

"I am Jenny. You are my brother. Your name is Billy," she answered with that same blank expression.

After several minutes of silence, Billy's mom rushed into the kitchen. "Okay, quickly, let's go! Come on! Come on!"

CHAPTER 2

They went to the school, and afterward, his mom drove all the way to his grandfather's old home. Jenny would be home early. Because she was entering the chess tournament, she didn't have regular class that day. Billy couldn't concentrate on his schoolwork. All he could think about was his sister.

When Aunt Bethany and Jenny picked him up after school, Billy studied the fake Jenny all the way home in the car. She seemed more like herself than in the morning. He began to wonder if it had just been his imagination or perhaps that she had been playing a trick on him.

When they arrived, Jenny headed straight into the living room, turned on the T.V., and hit play on the VCR.

His aunt whispered to him, "She's been watching those old home videos since we came back from the competition. Wouldn't say how it went either. I have a feeling it didn't go as well as she had hoped. Best to just leave it alone, I say. Let things work themselves out."

"Home videos?" Billy asked himself. This was not his sister. Whoever this is, is learning to be her. It's trying to become her. *"How can this be? And where is the real Jenny?"* he wondered.

"Sorry? You say something?" Bethany asked her nephew.

"Oh, no Auntie. I'm going to go up to my room for awhile. I have some homework I want to get done right away," he lied. He wanted to search Jenny's room. He wanted to find

< A Doorway Of Mirrors >   < By Katrina Mandrake-Johnston >   < 4 >

out what happened.

"Sure. Sounds like the perfect chance to read this book I've brought along with me. I've been dying to read it. I'll make some tea," she told him, "You want some? I could bring you up a cup of herbal."

"No, that's okay," Billy said bounding up the stairs.

Billy sat upon his sister's bed trying to think of what could have possibly happened to her. The clock began to chime. Billy thought nothing of it at first, until he happened to glance over at the full-length mirror on Jenny's wall. Each time the clock chimed, a ripple vibrated along the surface of the glass, as if someone had dropped a pebble into a pond of still water.

Curious, he stepped up to the mirror. Could this have something to do with Jenny's strange disappearance? The fake Jenny must have come from somewhere. Nervously, he outstretched his hand and touched the mirror.

It was completely normal. But then the clock made one last chime, and as the mirror rippled, his hand passed right through! He couldn't believe his eyes! It felt cold on the other side. The air was moist and icy breezes kept passing over his hand.

Billy pulled his hand back, afraid that it might become trapped within the mirror and especially now that the chimes had ceased. His hand appeared normal, as did the surface of the mirror, but his skin felt chilled. He stared in amazement from his hand to the mirror, back to his hand, and then finally to the old mysterious grandfather clock.

Could this be where his little sister had gone? Into the mirror?! The strange duplicate that was downstairs, right this minute, taking Jenny's place, had to be stopped! There had to be some way to rescue his sister!

Billy was afraid. If he passed through the mirror, would he be able to get back again? Would a duplicate of him pass through to take his place? What was to stop him from getting trapped just as Jenny did? How often did this gateway open? It was obviously somehow linked to the old clock. The clock belonged to his grandfather, but now that he was gone, there was no way to ask him if he knew of the mysterious powers it held. Plus, there wasn't time! Jenny was in terrible danger! He just knew it! Next time the gateway opened, he had to pass through and rescue her. He had to take the risk. He couldn't just sit by while the fake Jenny took her place.

If it did open the next time the clock chimed, Billy wanted to be ready. All he knew was that it was cold on the other side, so he went to his room and put on his thick blue sweater. He had no idea of what to bring with him. He had no idea of what to expect on the other side. Should he go back downstairs? He didn't want the fake Jenny to become suspicious.

Billy finally decided that if he were going to do this, he had better make some sort of rope to tether himself safely in this world, so he would be able to find his way back through the gateway. He stripped down his bed and began tying the sheets together. Then he proceeded to tie on several long-sleeved shirts and sweaters to make it even longer.

He carried his rope to his sister's room. All was quiet downstairs. Billy added Jenny's bed sheets as well to his rope and tied one end to the bed leg, and next, the other end tightly around his waist. By this time, the grandfather clock was close to striking the next hour.

CHAPTER 3

Billy took a deep breath and waited for the chimes to begin. He watched the pendulum swing back and forth, back and forth, and then the first loud and hollow chime came. The mirror rippled. Billy stepped up to the mirror and placed his hands upon the cool smooth surface.

On the second chime, Billy stepped into the mirror and gasped in amazement. He stood in the middle of an empty street. It was what someone would find in any typical neighborhood, although everything had a greyish tone to it, as if most of the color had been drained out of everything.

Billy checked the rope. It held firmly, and it seemed to be keeping the gateway open, as his hand had done before.

On one side of the street were houses, but they appeared abandoned and lifeless, as did the small shops along the opposite side of the street. An eerie and icy wind whistled down the street making Billy shiver.

There was complete silence here. Not even the chirp of a bird or the buzz of an insect could be heard here. But what was most odd in this place was that Billy couldn't smell anything. Usually, in any other neighborhood around this time of year, you would be able to catch a whiff of food cooking within the houses, sometimes of flowers from a garden, or the smell of freshly mowed grass. There would be at least something. Billy had never really been very aware of things like this until now. Now that not a sound or even a scent were here within the stale air of this place, he was all too aware of it. He could see the odd flower here and there in the yards, but they had no fragrance. It was as if only a dusty and stale residue was left here of everything. As if only a pale reminder of what should be was allowed to remain.

Then he heard footsteps drawing nearer and nearer to his location. Could it be Jenny? He was afraid to call out. Billy waited, and soon he was able to see that a tall skinny man was approaching him, walking slowly down the street.

He wore a black suit with a black flat-rimmed hat. One hand was behind his back and the other swung back and forth as he calmly came to meet Billy.

"Hello, and what might you be doing out here all alone?" the man asked Billy in a low melodious tone.

This man had a pale bony face and his dark eyes stared down at Billy from beneath the rim of his hat. His thin lips had the hint of a smile, that did not at all seem friendly. It made Billy feel as if this man had some devious plan for him and it made him feel very uncomfortable.

"Come now, boy. Don't you know it's rude not to answer when you have been asked a question?" the man asked him.

Billy didn't know what to do.

"What might that rope be for?" the man inquired, far too interested to Billy's liking. The man's dark beady eyes kept examining the rope and how it appeared to disappear into thin air where it met the gateway of the mirror.

"Where am I, sir?" Billy had the nerve to ask.

"What's this?" The man's smile widened into a toothy grin. "Don't know where you

< A Doorway Of Mirrors >   < By Katrina Mandrake-Johnston >   < 6 >

are? Oh, that's a shame, isn't it? Why don't I start by introducing myself. I'm assuming you know how to make a proper introduction, stating your name, accompanied by a firm and proper handshake?"

Billy didn't know what to do, but he felt he should say at least something and then hopefully this man would leave him alone. He said nervously, "My… my name's Billy."

The man stared intensely at him and cleared his throat. He was expecting Billy to extend his hand for the handshake.

Billy slowly put out his hand, even though he felt it was not a wise thing to do.

"That's a boy," the man grinned, "My name is not really important, as you will know me as your doom," the man said as he lashed out at Billy with his hand, the one that the man had kept hidden out of sight behind his back. It was not really a hand, as he had long purplish-white tentacles instead of fingers.

Luckily, Billy had been extremely wary of this strange man and leapt back through the portal before he could grab hold of him. But, just before Billy could fully escape him, one of the tentacle-like fingers touched his cheek. It stung and itched where it had touched him, just as if he had been stung by a bee.

Billy found himself back in Jenny's room. The mirror had returned to normal, and Billy could see a dark purple mark where the tentacle had touched him. The mark began to fade, and after a few moments, it had completely vanished.

Who was that horrible man? Did Jenny run into him when she entered? Was she trapped in that horrible place with no way of getting back again? That man is evil, whoever he is. Billy had to go back. He couldn't leave Jenny there! She was in terrible danger! He had to rescue her!

CHAPTER 4

"Billy? You up there? Come say good-bye to Auntie Bethany," his mother called from downstairs.

"Yes, Mum," he answered, untying his rope from around his waist. He quickly ran to his room to store it for later. He wondered if the fake Jenny would be suspicious of the missing bed sheets. He would have to put them back before bedtime. Would his mother realize that it was not the real Jenny? Billy went downstairs to greet his mom and to say good-bye to his aunt.

Once his aunt had left, his mother sighed and announced that she needed a strong cup of tea. Billy sat down at the kitchen table and glanced over to the living room where the imposter was still watching the videos.

"So how'd it go at Grandpa's?" Billy asked, as his mom prepared the tea.

"Oh, all right I guess. There's so much more to go through though. Oh, I brought a few things back with me that I thought you might like," she told him.

"So did Grandpa ever say anything about the old clock?" Billy asked, hoping to learn something that could help him.

"No, not really. What sort of things?" she said taking a sip of her tea.

"Well, I don't know. Just anything special about it," said Billy.

"Well most other grandfather clocks play a little tune with their chimes, playing more of the tune, the more the hours progress. That old thing just has a plain old dull one over and over again. If you ask me, I'd far prefer the other kind," she said taking another sip of tea and leaning up against the kitchen counter, "Why are you so interested? I thought it was Jenny that was nuts about that thing. Don't tell me you want it moved into your room now."

< A Doorway Of Mirrors >   < By Katrina Mandrake-Johnston >   < 7 >

"Oh, no, it's nothing I guess," he told her.

"I really don't feel like cooking anything for dinner, so how's about we order in pizza? It'll be a special treat," his mother suggested with a warm smile.

"Pizza?! Yeah, great! Thanks Mom!" Billy said, as pizza was one of his favorite foods, especially if it came with extra cheese.

"I think Jenny's feeling a little depressed. You know, with Grandpa passing on, and I don't think she did too well in the chess competition. Most of the kids entering were at least a few years older than her. She's apparently been in there staring at home movies for hours. She'll hopefully cheer up when the pizza gets here. I think we all need a bit of a pick-me-up," said his mom as she flipped through the phone book.

Billy reminded her, "You said there were some things for me from Grandpa's?"

"Oh, they're just in that bag over there by the door. Why don't you take them up to your room," she suggested, "Pizza will be a long while as they're usually pretty backed up with orders for the dinner rush."

"Okay, thanks Mum," Billy said, snatching up the bag and heading up the stairs to his room.

He first untied the sheets he used from Jenny's room and put them back as quickly as he could. He didn't want the imposter to know that he had been in there.

CHAPTER 5

Once back in his room, he opened up the plastic bag and emptied out its contents. There was a watch that needed repairs, a couple of old coins, and a few other odd trinkets, but what was most interesting was a small and very worn black book. The cover read "The Adventures of…" and then the rest Billy couldn't make out.

Billy opened the book and flipped through the dusty yellowed pages. He was amazed to discover that the last half of the book had been hollowed out and that an odd looking key had been placed within. Curious, Billy removed it and marveled at the colorful crystals that were embedded in the metal of the key. A note was beneath in the hollow and Billy carefully unfolded the fragile paper.

If you are reading this, a most terrible thing has occurred. I have become trapped within the other world, and an imposter has taken my place. I assure you, I am quite sane.

I have seen this happen, and no doubt, the inconsistencies my double will possess will be seen as the effects of old age. It seems that my attempts to rescue the others have failed, and I too have become captured.

I left behind my key to the dimensional gateway and have left via the grandfather clock. I have left behind several other tools that could be useful in the other world, but the clues to what they are and their location, I have left within the other world for safety reasons, as I have no guarantee that whomever is reading this is friend or foe. Use the key wisely, as there are a lot of people, myself included now, that are counting on your survival and your ability to rescue us.

Beware the man with no name and his devilish hand. I've seen him drain the very essence out of a person, turning them into slaves, and then use his powers to send a double into our world to trick others through the mirrors for him to prey upon.

All is not lost for those he drains, as their energy is crystallized into jewel-like

< A Doorway Of Mirrors >   < By Katrina Mandrake-Johnston >   < 8 >

*objects and he keeps these guarded in several different locations within the other world. I
hope to rescue these people if I can, but it seems I have failed.*
Good luck my friend, if you decide to follow me in this quest.

       Billy stared in astonishment at the paper he held in his hand. His grandfather was still
alive? For how long did his duplicate take his place? He seemed to be himself right to the
end, except for being a little forgetful at times. Maybe it was true.

       Billy had met the man with no name and was now even more thankful that he had
escaped him. Was Jenny now a slave to this horrible man? Did he drain out her essence? If
so, he had to find the crystal that contained it and somehow restore his sister to her former self.

       What could have happened to his grandfather? Since imposters were sent forth into
this world for both his grandfather and his sister, it must mean that the man with no name had
captured them. It would be dangerous, but he had to try to help them. He had to figure out
how to work this mysterious key.

CHAPTER 6

       There was better light in the bathroom and he brought the key there so he could
examine it better. Standing before the sink, Billy held the mysterious key up to the light. The
colorful crystals sparkled and shimmered, all different wondrous shades of blue, green, and
red.

       Billy wondered if there were perhaps some sort of keyhole for it to fit into, and as he
stood there holding the key, the bathroom mirror over the sink began to ripple just as the one in
Jenny's room had done with the chimes of the clock. Billy was amazed.

       Could this key open a gateway to the other world simply by being close to a mirror?
Was there a way to keep the gateway open with this key and keep him from becoming trapped?
Or was it possible to open a gateway back in the same way using the key from the other side?

       Surely the man with no name must have smashed every mirror within that world.
Perhaps he didn't know how the portal worked. He seemed awfully curious when Billy had
first entered. He needed new people to become his slaves, but maybe he didn't know exactly
how they came to the other world. That would mean the imposters were unable to contact the
man with no name once they came over to this side.

       If Billy went back in, would he come out in the same place he had the first time or
somewhere different? Would the man with no name be waiting for him? If only his
grandfather had written more in his note…

       Billy held out the key, pointing it toward the mirror. "There's only one way to find
out," he said to himself.

       The key began to vibrate, the mirror started to ripple more rapidly, and a force began
to draw Billy and the key forward toward the mirror and the gateway.

       "Billy!" his mother called from downstairs, "The pizza's here!"

       He would have to wait. He couldn't pass up pizza. It was one of his favorite foods.
Besides, once on the other side, he wasn't sure if he could get back, and he doubted they had
pizza there.

CHAPTER 7

       When Billy came downstairs into the kitchen, Jenny was sitting at the kitchen table.
If he didn't know better, he would have sworn that it was the real Jenny. It would be
impossible for his mother to tell the difference. The imposter that had replaced their

< A Doorway Of Mirrors >   < By Katrina Mandrake-Johnston >   < 9 >

grandfather had them all fooled for years, and now Jenny's imposter knew enough from the videos to copy her behavior. If Billy hadn't discovered the truth about her, he would have been fooled along with everybody else.

The pizza smelled wonderful. Billy sat down and took two cheesy pieces out of the box to put onto his plate.

"Don't forget the napkins," his mom reminded them, "The last thing I want is greasy fingers all over the house."

Jenny took a piece of the ham and pineapple pizza and placed it on her plate as Billy had done. Billy had already taken three large bites of his pizza. It was delicious and the cheese was warm and gooey. Jenny took a bite and immediately spit it out with a disgusted look on her face.

"Jenny! What are you doing?!" Billy's mom exclaimed, "I got the right kind, didn't I?"

"Yes Mom, ham and pineapple with extra cheese. It's Jenny's favorite and mine too," Billy explained taking another big bite.

"Yes, sorry Mom," the imposter said, "It was just a little too hot at first."

She took a second bite and pretended that she liked it. Billy knew the truth. But wait, he had just helped her by saying it was their favorite! He had just helped the imposter learn yet another piece of information about Jenny! Pretty soon there wouldn't be anything left to help determine the real Jenny from the fake one. He had to rescue his sister.

Billy just then had a horrible thought. What if the man with no name had drained enough of his essence with that one slight touch of his tentacle hand? What if he were already able to make a duplicate of Billy? He couldn't allow that to happen. He was afraid to leave his mom here all alone with this strange being that had taken his sister's place, but he had to go through the mirror. He couldn't wait any longer.

"I'm going to go to bed early. I'm feeling a little sick, Mom," Billy told her, stuffing the last of his pizza into his mouth and grabbing up the other piece to take with him.

"Hey, wait a minute," his mom said, "Don't forget a napkin. I'm going to go to bed early too. I've got to go back to Grandpa's tomorrow. Hopefully Aunt Bethany will be able to watch you two. Looks like Dad is going to be home late again. I'll have to save some pizza for him. Jenny, I want you in bed right after dinner. You look like you're coming down with Dad's cold."

"I'm probably going to be asleep for most of the day, Mom," Billy said faking a cough.

"Alright, I'll phone you in sick to the school tomorrow, and I'll also tell Bethany just to let you sleep when she brings Jenny home and not to bother you. Make sure you brush your teeth before bed," his mother smiled at him, "And you better not be up to something, you have that look you get."

"Okay," said Billy finishing up his pizza as he climbed the stairs.

Did his mom know more than she was letting on? She was the one who had brought the book back with the key inside. Did she suspect there was something wrong with Jenny?

"*Probably not,*" Billy decided and went to the bathroom where he had left the key.

He dropped his napkin into the wastebasket, picked up the key, and pointed it toward the mirror. It began to vibrate with power, the mirror rippled madly, and a force began to pull Billy into it. Billy climbed up on the bathroom counter, and firmly holding onto the key, crawled inside through the gateway.

< A Doorway Of Mirrors >   < By Katrina Mandrake-Johnston >   < 10 >

CHAPTER 8

Billy found himself in the dark and felt with his hands that there were walls all around him. At first he had no idea of where he might be, and then, he began to realize that he was inside a cardboard box.

He pushed his way out, and as he stood, he found himself to be in a small shop with many boxes, large and small, piled high and also scattered about the floor. The air here was so very stale and everything had that same dull greyness that it had when Billy had come through into this world the first time.

He carefully pocketed the key and began to look around. He tried the front door but found it tightly locked and could hear the rattle of chains holding it shut from the outside. Was he in one of the shops he had seen from the street when he had encountered the man with no name?

The small window beside the door had been boarded up from the outside as well, and only a small amount of light was able to illuminate the shop through the cracks between the boards.

There didn't seem to be any way out of this place. He checked the box he had come out of, even tried using the key there, but nothing happened and there was no gateway now.

Billy let out a frustrated sigh. How was he supposed to rescue his sister now, if he had become trapped himself within this shop? Billy heard a dry raspy cough.

"Is someone there?" Billy said nervously.

CHAPTER 9

"Eh? What?" a voice said, "Somebody out there? I say, would you mind moving some of these boxes out of the way? I can't see a darn thing."

Billy started moving the boxes away from where he believed the voice to have come from. Besides the empty boxes he had moved, all that was in this part of the room was an old coo-coo clock and only the numbers 10, 2, and 6 remained on its face.

Billy was about to start searching in another part of the store, but then he heard the voice again and Billy was certain that it was coming from the old clock. "Why Johnny Tom Tom! I hadn't expected to see you again! It's been awhile, I can tell you that! Where abouts are my spectacles? Do you see them Johnny?"

Billy looked around and noticed that on top of one of the larger boxes rested a tiny pair of glasses. He felt incredibly foolish, but he presented them to the coo-coo clock.

"Are these them? My name is not Johnny; it's Billy."

"Wonderful! You've found them!" the clock exclaimed, and suddenly a little blue bird shot out from behind two little doors near the top of the clock and plucked the glasses from Billy's hand. Next the bird dropped them down onto the face of the clock, positioning

< A Doorway Of Mirrors >   < By Katrina Mandrake-Johnston >   < 11 >

them as if the numbers 10 and 2 were eyes, and then popped back through the tiny doors once more. "Oh thank-you! That's much better. Not Johnny? Billy, you say your name is? But I could have sworn that you were him."

"My grandfather's name was John. Perhaps I look a bit like him," Billy suggested, hoping this strange clock might be able to give him some useful information.

"Grandfather?!" the clock exclaimed, "That much time couldn't have possibly gone by already. Oh, well, it might have. You see, I've never been one for keeping track of time very well. I know, I am a clock, and one would think I tell time very well, but alas, this is not the case. I suppose this is why I ended up here."

Billy asked excitedly, "So you knew my grandfather then?"

"Oh, once upon a time. I remember he used to have grand adventures here as a boy," the clock told him, "Things used to be different then. Now, since that awful man came, everything is so grey. So many have become slaves and those in hiding are too frightened to do anything about it. He does whatever he likes to our world and is slowly changing it into a terrible place. Even the land and vegetation are being mutated to suit his liking. Where peaceful creatures once roamed, now horrid monsters lurk as he has changed them into such. Johnny was always saying that he wasn't going to stand for such wickedness much longer and that he was going to do something to stop the man with no name. Perhaps he tried and failed."

"Is there anything I can do?" Billy asked, "I need to rescue my sister, and my grandfather is trapped here as well. Do you know where they might be? This is why I am here."

"Oh, no. I do not know of such things and it seems that I have been here far too long to be of any help to you," the clock explained, "I can tell you, however, that you should not go about such a task so blindly. The man with no name is an incredible foe. It will not be simply a matter of finding your family."

Billy was beginning to lose hope. "But I don't know what I should do!"

"Then learn, dear boy," the clock replied.

"I can't even get out of here!" Billy told him.

"Oh wait, if I remember correctly, I may know of something that could help you. Not that long ago, or maybe it was ages ago, it could be, an odd little fellow was also imprisoned here. He's small, no bigger than your hand, and flat, but rounded in the middle. See if you can find him," the clock said to Billy, as the little bird popped out and adjusted his spectacles.

Billy searched and searched for what seemed like hours without success. Then something shiny fell out from one of the boxes and skidded across the floor.

"That's him! That's him!" the clock exclaimed with excitement, "Well, what are you waiting for? Go after him, boy!"

Billy followed where the object had gone. When he picked it up and held it in his hand, suddenly, it came to life. Two little metallic eyes rose up from its surface and it made a soft clicking sound.

"Bring him close, Billy," the clock instructed. Billy brought the strange little object

< A Doorway Of Mirrors >   < By Katrina Mandrake-Johnston >   < 18 >

and opened the box. Inside was a tightly rolled piece of paper. Perhaps it was a message from his grandfather! His note from before, in the book with the key, had said that there would be clues to important tools in Billy's world that he could bring across. Could this be one? And would he even be able to get back to his own world to search for whatever the clues were meant for?

Billy carefully unfolded the paper. The slithering sound was getting louder. The serpent creature was coming back along the corridor! Billy read quickly.

A broken bottle…all a mottle…can allow you to see…where a passage may be.

Billy took out the key, and the mirror began to vibrate again, but quietly this time. The beast was coming to check his room. He had to move fast! If it saw Billy escape through a mirror, the man with no name would surely order all the mirrors in this world destroyed. Billy quickly climbed through the mirror, and a few moments after, the panel slid back to reveal an empty room to the astonished guard.

CHAPTER 17

Billy found himself to be standing in the middle of the hall in his house. Downstairs, he could see his mother in the kitchen standing over the table. He ducked behind the wall and peered around the corner. Down in the kitchen, he could see Jenny, and there was a boy also seated there with his back to Billy. Billy stayed out of sight, but he thought his mom might have seen him when he had first emerged from the portal.

"*Who is the boy?*" Billy wondered, "*Oh no, could it be an imposter of me?*"

"Billy?" his mother said, speaking to the boy, "I've brought some more things back from Grandpa's. I've left them in my room in a bag on my bed."

The fake Billy eagerly stood up from the table. "No, no," his mom said putting her hand onto the boy's shoulder, "Sit back down. You have to finish your dinner. You'll have plenty of time later."

"*Did she just look nervously toward the top of the stairs? Did she somehow know? How could she?*" Billy wondered, "*And dinner? How long was I in the other world?! It looks as if it were all night and all the way through until supper the next day!*"

Billy crept into his mother's room. On her bed was a plastic bag, but Billy was more curious about her big oval mirror hanging on the wall. It seemed to shimmer with a strange light that Billy had never noticed before. Billy stepped up to the mirror and he could see that shapes were beginning to form within.

Soon, the images were as clear as if he were peering through a window. It was Squeeshna! She was leaping from tree to tree, and below her, two large wolf-like beasts with bright red eyes and huge teeth were chasing her. Billy marveled again at how quick and limber she could be, and soon she had escaped far way from the creatures. It would be awhile, perhaps a few days, before she could return to her home undetected.

Had his mother seen through the mirror what had happened to him? Had she known all along? She had said that she was going to bed early that night. Was it to watch over him in the mirror? She had reminded him to brush his teeth. Had she said this to guide him to the bathroom mirror? She must have seen him return just now and was keeping the imposters from finding him. It would only be until the other Billy was finished dinner, but he hoped his mom would get both the imposters to wash the dishes and give him more time.

Billy poured the contents of the bag out onto the bed. There were two identical cat statues, a fan, a cloth handkerchief with the letter 'R' embroidered into it, and a round thick piece of glass. Billy held the glass up to his eye and it appeared to distort everything he saw

< A Doorway Of Mirrors >   < By Katrina Mandrake-Johnston >   < 19 >
through it.

"Oh, do you remember Grandpa's cat Tom? It was a long time ago, but he always used to talk about him," his mother said loudly from downstairs.

Why would his mom want him to hear that? The clock had called him Johnny Tom Tom. Billy had thought it had just been a silly nickname, but perhaps it was a clue. His mom obviously thought so, as she brought these two cats back from Grandpa's house. This piece of glass must be the answer to the riddle Grandpa left in the Ivory Palace.

But wait a minute, when did his mom have a chance to get these things? She could have gone to get the cat statues when he had been recovering from the poison, but for the glass? He just got the note a few moments ago before he entered the mirror. Perhaps it took longer than he thought to travel through the gateways. To him, it seemed as if it had been but a second from one side to the other, but it must have been several hours. This was lucky for Billy, as it had given his mom enough time to get the items from his grandfather's and have the imposters occupied before he returned.

Billy pocketed the glass and picked up the two cats. He looked them over and over, and then he saw that there was a tiny hole in each side of the cats and that, if he were able to entwine the tails a certain way, he would be able to fit the tail ends into the holes like two keys into their locks. Billy fiddled around with them without success.

"But Billy!" his mom called loudly, "Don't you want dessert? It's apple pie, your favorite!"

"No, Mom," the imposter said, coming up the stairs.

Billy finally got the puzzle to fit. The bottoms of the statues opened, a colorful marble falling out of each.

Billy scooped them up and hid under his mother's bed just as the imposter opened the door and walked in.

Billy lay very still. The imposter stepped up to the bed, and Billy heard the clink of him picking up the cat statues and then, a few moments later, of dropping them back onto the bed.

Was he suspicious? Did he know that Billy was still here somewhere in the room? Billy watched the fake Billy's feet move away from the bed and walk up to the magical mirror. He smashed it to bits! "Sorry, Mom!" the imposter called out, "I tripped and broke your mirror!"

Billy's mom rushed in. "Oh no! How could you?!" his mother wailed. Billy thought she were about to cry by the sound of her voice. "Please, get out of my room," she told the imposter.

"But Mom, the items," he reminded.

"Not now. I have to clean up the glass. Please get out. I… I don't want you to hurt yourself," she tried to convince him.

Billy's mom closed the door behind the fake Billy. The real Billy crawled out from under the bed and quietly hugged his mother. They couldn't say a word or the imposters would know.

She opened her bottom drawer and took out several square pieces of mirror. She then placed them on the floor and they magically melded together into one. Billy took out Click to show him to her, but when he opened his hand, he held only a rock. It looked as if it were

< A Doorway Of Mirrors >   < By Katrina Mandrake-Johnston >   < 20 >

impossible to bring back anything that belonged within the other world. He put the rock back into his pocket, and his mom hurried Billy over to the mirror.

She had fooled the imposters into thinking she didn't know so far, but how long until they found her out? Would they eventually force her through one of the mirrors to become a slave and replace her with a duplicate as well? He had to hurry.

She kissed him good-bye with tears in her eyes, and Billy, using the key, went through the doorway of mirrors she had created for him. He was on his own now in this.

CHAPTER 18

Billy found himself back in the Ivory Palace, but this time within a long white corridor and not in a prison cell as before. The corridor seemed to go on and on forever. He could not see the end of the passageway or any twists or turns. Billy turned around to look behind him and it was the same in the other direction. There weren't any doors. There weren't any markings of any kind. All that Billy could see were smooth seamless white walls, ceiling, and floor.

Billy listened nervously for the slithering sound the reptilian creature made that he had heard before from within the prison cell. There was no sound, but Billy knew that he must be in one of the passageways that the creature guarded.

He emptied his pockets. He had the key, the two marbles from the cat statues, the round piece of warped glass, and Click. Click had appeared as a mere rock back in his world, but now that he had returned, Click was back to normal.

"How are you doing, Click?" Billy whispered, "Are you okay?"

"Buzz click click," he told him. Click was all right.

Click's answer echoed loudly down the corridor and Billy decided not to ask Click anything else unless it were an emergency. He didn't want to alert the guard.

Billy took the piece of glass and held it up to his eye. At first, everything looked the same as it had before, but then outlines of doors began to appear and parts of the walls fell away to reveal passageways off to the right and left of the corridor.

He took the glass away from his eye. Everything looked as it had before; it was just a long corridor with smooth walls and nothing more.

Billy held the glass up again so he was able to see through the illusion. Two doors on either side were just in front of him. Past these along the corridor, a passageway led off to the right and then, farther up, another passageway led to the left. Everything beyond this was blurred over and Billy would have to move closer to see more.

He looked behind him with the glass and was surprised to see a wall there instead of another corridor as he had thought before. There was only one direction for him to go in and that was forward. But there were so many choices and this was such a dangerous place.

"Should I try the door on the…" Billy began and then stopped himself. If he asked Click what to do, the guard would hear. He had to make the decision on his own.

"*A room is probably best to check first,*" Billy decided, "*That way I won't get too lost right away. I'll just take a quick look around the room and then I'll know exactly where I am when I come out again. But what if there are more doors inside the room leading in other directions?*

"*I'm going to get hopelessly lost! I don't even know what I am looking for here! A way out? I still won't have a clue of where I am or where to go if I get out of here.*

"*And what about my mom? What happened before doesn't seem as scary now that I know my mom was watching over me through her mirror. Did she ever come here? Grandpa did for*

< A Doorway Of Mirrors >   < By Katrina Mandrake-Johnston >   < 21 >

sure. Mom seemed to know exactly where the portal would be letting out. Maybe she was too young to go with Grandpa to this world when it had become such a dangerous place, but she was probably old enough back then to help him in the same way that she had helped me.

"But now I am all alone! No one knows where I am. No one would know if I end up in danger. Back in my home world, the fake me would take over my entire life, and my friends wouldn't know the difference. No one would ever believe that something like this could happen! To everyone else, my family is just going through regular days doing our everyday boring activities, not being slowly replaced by imposters from a different world! What can I possibly do?! I'm just a little kid!"

All of a sudden, Billy got an electric shock. He pulled out the marbles, and as he held them out in his palm, an arc of electricity jumped between them and then out toward the wall. Billy stared in amazement at the two marbles he held. They had returned to normal now and Billy wondered what had just happened.

He looked to where the lightening-like bolt had struck the wall. He was thankful that only a faint crackling sound had occurred during all this. Billy was sure the guard was lurking around in here somewhere. On the wall, parts of it were starting to glow with a strange blue light.

Soon Billy was able to read the word 'LEARN' and below it the word 'TRY'. Billy realized that this was true. He had to try. No one else would be able to save his family. He had to learn what to do. No one was going to show him. No one was going to accomplish this rescue for him. He had to find out what to do on his own. He hoped others would be able to help him, like Squeeshna might be able to with her efforts to restore the slaves back to normal, but he couldn't expect to sit idly by while others faced the danger for him.

He peered through the glass and finally made a decision to try the door on the left.

CHAPTER 19

Inside the room Billy entered, there were shelves all along the walls from the floor to

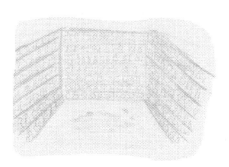

the ceiling and the room had a musty smell to it. On the shelves were numerous bottles, all of which were covered in a thick layer of dust. In the middle of the floor was a dark blue stain and there were shards of broken glass around it. Someone must have smashed one of the bottles.

Billy wondered who could have done this and what had been in the bottle. Why were these here? There were so many of them!

Billy wanted to ask Click about the bottles. He could, now that they were out of the corridors. The guard wouldn't be able to hear, as Billy had closed the door behind him. But what could he possibly ask Click? He could only answer yes or no, not tell him what was in them or what they could be used for. Billy thought for quite awhile about what he might be able to learn from Click here. He couldn't take the time to ask him if he should or shouldn't take each bottle; there were too many. Even if he could, Billy wouldn't know what to do with the bottles afterwards if he did take some.

"Click," he whispered taking him out, "Did the man with no name want this bottle destroyed?"

Click looked around the room, his little metallic eyes searching all around. It took

< A Doorway Of Mirrors >   < By Katrina Mandrake-Johnston >   < 22 >

him a little while, but finally he answered, "Buzz buzz."

  "That means no," Billy thought to himself, *"Who could have done it then?"*

  "Was it an accident?" he asked Click, and he replied no again.

  "My grandfather?" Billy wondered, and Click told him no.

  "Is the person who broke the bottle here in the Ivory Palace?" Billy hoped.

  Click tucked his little eyes back into his body and Billy became a little worried.

  "Click?" he whispered.

  Click began to shake and his little metal body started to heat up. Billy could hear a whirring and snapping sound, like gears that were being wound too tightly.

  "Click?" Billy said again, with worry and fear for his little friend.

  "I've been asking him questions that are way too hard for him, things that he couldn't possibly know. It's all my fault! I should never have expected the poor little guy to answer all of my questions for me! Squeeshna was right. I said I was returning for him because he was my friend, but here I am asking him all these difficult questions hoping he will make things easier for me. I've broken him! I've destroyed my little friend! He saved my life, directing me through the tunnels away from the prickly monster that surely would have gotten me. I probably wouldn't have even gotten out of the shop had Click not been there. What have I done?!"

  Little streams of black smoke began to seep out from where his eyes should be.

  "Click, no!" he wailed, "I'm sorry! Please, I don't want to know the answer! Please! Be okay, please! I'm sorry!"

  Click became still. The smoke dispersed.

  "Click! Don't be dead! Please!" Billy said to his dear little friend.

  Billy stood there with tears streaming down his face, as he stared at poor Click resting in his palm. He stood there within the complete silence of the room, trying to think of what he could possibly do. Each minute that passed felt to him like hours, his heart aching with sadness.

  Billy heard a soft whirring sound and Click's eyes popped up and spun around to look at Billy. "Buzz click click," he answered.

  "You're alive!" Billy exclaimed smiling down at him.

  Whoever had smashed the bottle was still here in the Ivory Palace, but this information had almost cost Click his life.

  "I'm so glad you're all right," Billy told him, wiping away his tears, "I thought I lost you. I'm so sorry. Shall we go search the other room then? Do you feel okay?"

  Click said that he was, and Billy slipped him safely back into his pocket.

CHAPTER 20

  Billy stuck his head out into the corridor, and using his glass piece, looked nervously around for the guard. He hurried across to the other door and pulled on the handle. It opened easily and Billy stepped into a dark room. The only light was that which was coming in through the open door.

  He saw something move in the corner of the room. It was big. Billy saw spines. Billy slowly started to back out of the room.

  Could it be a larger version of the creature he encountered in the tunnels? He would never be able to outrun it! Billy continued to carefully and quietly exit the room, fearing that two large yellow eyes would soon lock onto him. Squeeshna had saved him from the poisonous spines of the smaller one, but Billy would never survive an attack from this one!

< A Doorway Of Mirrors >   < By Katrina Mandrake-Johnston >   < 23 >

The creature was moving! Billy's heart began to pound hard and fast with fear.

Then he saw a pink nose on the end of a furry snout come into the light. Then Billy saw two black little eyes come into view and, behind them, two fuzzy mouse-like ears. Billy got ready to run if he had to. The spines he had seen in the darkness were on this creature's back, like that of a hedgehog. It had rolled itself into a ball of prickly spines for protection and that was what Billy had seen.

"Who are you?" the creature asked stepping forward, its little nails making a soft clicking sound against the floor as it walked, "Are you here to free me?"

"I… I suppose," Billy said, astonished that the creature had spoken, but he was slowly becoming more and more accustomed to it now, especially after encountering the coo-coo clock and Squeeshna.

"Really?" it exclaimed in delight, "Oh, it has been so long! My name is Rashnin, and I was imprisoned here by that foul monster known as the man with no name. He has made many attempts to transform me into one of his slaves, but he is unable to accomplish this because of my spines. He locked me in here, hoping that with time I would reveal information about those who have so far eluded him. He has denied me food and water, but I have been surviving within a hibernation-like state until your entry just now. I assume you have means of seeing beyond the illusion of this place or you would not have been able to find me here. There is a guard who occasionally comes to check on the prisoners. He is a reptilian beast who is loyal to the man with no name. He devours any prisoners the man with no name instructs him to and those that are able to escape their cells. He has the tail of a great serpent, the talons of a bird of prey, and the powerful jaws of a crocodile. If we are to escape, we must stay clear of this beast. We may be able to hear him moving along the passageways, but we must move swiftly."

Billy nodded, and Rashnin, who was as large as Billy, followed him into the corridor.

CHAPTER 21

"Do you know the way out, Rashnin?" Billy asked.

"No, but I may be able to find it... well, perhaps. I have a good sense of smell. It may help," he replied.

"My name's Billy. My sister and grandfather were captured. I'm trying to save them," he told the hedgehog-like being.

"A difficult task indeed," he commented.

"What about others? Are there other prisoners here?" Billy asked, looking around the corridor through the glass piece.

"It's likely," Rashnin replied, "I do not know for sure, however."

"There's a passage to the right and another to the left," Billy told him, "Which way do you want to try?"

"Wait, Billy. Listen," said Rashnin, "Do you hear that?"

Billy listened, but heard nothing. "No," he whispered.

"It's coming!" Rashnin said with fear as he rolled himself into a prickly ball.

"You can't hide here!" Billy told him frantically, "We have to escape!"

"I'm frightened! It may not be able to devour me if I hide like this. Run, save yourself!" Rashnin told him, his voice trembling.

"No! You have to come too! I need your help!" Billy pleaded.

< A Doorway Of Mirrors >   < By Katrina Mandrake-Johnston >   < 24 >

Billy heard the slithering sound of the guard approaching.

CHAPTER 22

"No, I can't!" Rashnin told him.

Things were starting to change around them. Everything that had been hidden by an illusion was now becoming visible. Billy could see the beast side-winding down a passageway toward them, its large jaws snapping eagerly as it approached. It had seen them and would be upon them within seconds. A deadly looking spear was clutched in its talons.

Billy shouted urgently at Rashnin, "It has a spear! It will stick you with it! Your spines won't protect you!"

Rashnin uncurled and sped off down the corridor running from the creature as fast as his little legs could carry him. Billy followed, his heart pounding hard in his chest. This was something out of a nightmare! Billy couldn't believe that this could be real!

Rashnin pushed open a large door with his little paw, and he and Billy ran inside. The room was huge and an enormous stone statue of a winged dragon was in the far corner. On one wall was an oval mirror that was at least double the size of Billy in height and near five feet across.

The mirror was a way out for Billy, but not for Rashnin. There wasn't near enough time for him to make his escape this way before the creature was upon them anyway. If Billy returned to his own world, what then? With the imposters lurking about and with no further clues to objects his grandfather left behind, going back there would be useless right now.

There was no way out of this room except for the way they came in and the creature was close behind. They had to hide somehow! It was their only chance!

"We might be able to squeeze behind the statue. Quick! Hurry!" Billy whispered to Rashnin whose eyes were madly searching the room in a panic.

They ran over to the statue and wriggled in between it and the wall. It was a tight fit, but they had managed it.

The creature slithered into the room, stopping in the middle as it inspected the empty room. Billy was afraid to even breathe he was so scared. What would happen if it found them? Just then one of Rashnin's sharp spines accidentally brushed up against Billy giving him a needle-like prick that made him utter a sound.

The guard twitched its head toward the dragon statue. Had it heard him? Billy felt hot tears roll down his cheeks. The creature was going to eat him! Billy had seen crocodiles

< A Doorway Of Mirrors >   < By Katrina Mandrake-Johnston >   < 25 >
eat chunks of meat in nature shows on T.V. Billy could think of nothing worse. He wanted all this to be just a crazy dream, but he knew that it wasn't, no matter how much it seemed like it.

The creature stayed where it was, adjusting its grip along the shaft of the spear, as if it were deciding what to do next. Maybe it was waiting for them to make another sound and reveal their location once more.

CHAPTER 23

Billy and Rashnin remained very still in their cramped position behind the statue, and finally, after quite some time had passed, the beast slithered away out the door. Perhaps the fact that Billy had confused it earlier within his prison cell by mysteriously disappearing as he had done helped them to escape the creature just now.

Rashnin and Billy remained where they were even longer, just to be sure that the beast wasn't still watching and hoping to trick them into coming out into the open. Soon after, they emerged.

"What do we do now?" Rashnin whispered.

"I guess we continue to look for a way out," Billy said bravely.

"That thing almost got us!" Rashnin exclaimed, "We can't go searching around with that monster out there!"

Billy walked up to the mirror. *"Perhaps I should go through. Anything is better than being eaten by a horrible creature like that, right? Maybe Rashnin could come too. I would just have to find some way of getting him back again and hope the imposters don't capture me before then,"* Billy reasoned with himself, staring up into the mirror, *"What if when we come back into this world, we come out in a far worse place than this? My mom went to all that trouble to send me here. Maybe that mirror she created out of the pieces was the only safe gateway left. The bathroom mirror took me into the shop which had been made into a prison. The one in Jenny's room led to an empty street within the grey domain of the man with no name, in the middle of nowhere it seemed."*

"Rashnin?" Billy said, "Did you ever come across a room full of bottles?"

"No, I can't say that I have. Why?" said Rashnin.

"That means someone else is trapped in here then," said Billy.

"Billy! The mirror! I can feel fresh air!" he told him excitedly, "I think it's a way out! A door, perhaps, disguised? Billy, can you check?"

"Really?" Billy said feeling around the edges of the mirror frame, "Hey, I feel it too!"

"Billy, hurry! I think the creature is coming back this way!" he warned him.

Billy pushed as hard as he could and it started to budge. It was a door! Rashnin put his front paws up onto the bottom of the frame and pushed as best as he was able to. As soon as the door was open enough for them to squeeze through, they were out. A vast field of lush green grass lay before them.

"Quickly, Billy, follow me," Rashnin instructed, "I'll take you to the others."

CHAPTER 24

"Others?" Billy questioned.

"Yes, the others. There are many of us in hiding," he explained, "I shall take you to the nearest encampment. We will be safe there, but we have to move quickly."

Billy nodded and followed Rashnin as they began to travel across the field. He felt guilty leaving when he knew someone else might still be imprisoned there, but Rashnin was right; it was far too dangerous to go back in with the creature about.

"Billy?" Rashnin asked, "You said something about your sister and grandfather?

< A Doorway Of Mirrors >   < By Katrina Mandrake-Johnston >   < 26 >

That they were captured?"

"Yes, at least I think they were. They're trapped here in this world somewhere," Billy told him.

Rashnin inquired, "You are from a different world than ours, aren't you?"

Billy nodded and explained, "The man with no name has replaced my sister and even myself with imposters; duplicates to take our place in our world. My mom knows what's going on. She even had a magic mirror that acted like a window into this world. I thought I just had a regular normal mom like everybody else until now. My grandpa too. An old coo-coo clock told me that he used to come here to play as a boy even."

"May I ask you a few questions? What is your grandfather's name?" he asked Billy.

"John," he answered.

"And your grandmother, you never met her?" Rashnin asked.

"No. I think she might have died before I was born," Billy told him, "Why?"

He said, "Just answer my questions for a minute."

"Alright," Billy said timidly, becoming more and more curious.

"So," Rashnin began, his spines rustling the tall grass around him as they walked, "Do you remember your mother or grandfather ever talking much about her?"

"Not really. A few things now and then, I suppose," Billy said wondering why the strange hedgehog-like being would be interested in such a bizarre thing.

"Do you remember ever seeing a picture of her?" he asked.

"Why? I don't think so. Probably when I was younger. I don't really remember though," Billy explained, "There are probably tons at my grandpa's house."

Rashnin sniffed the air and said, "This way now. Come on, and we must hurry. We must be extremely careful in traveling to the encampment. Its location must be kept a secret. The man with no name has many spies. So, can you think really hard for me? Think back, do you remember ever seeing a picture of her even at your grandfather's house? Don't just assume you have. Really try to remember."

"But why is this so important?" Billy questioned.

"I will tell you in a minute. I just need you to think back for me," Rashnin told him.

Billy tried to remember. He visualized each room in his grandfather's house and tried to recall what was there. All the shelves and tabletops flashed through his mind. Could it be that he had never seen one of her? And why was Rashnin so curious about this?

"You know," Billy realized in amazement, "I don't think I ever have. Not at my own house or my grandpa's."

"I thought so," Rashnin commented, "I think there's someone you should meet then. We'll be at the encampment soon."

CHAPTER   25

They eventually came to a wooded area and Rashnin led Billy in. Birds chirped their happy little songs. Tiny animals scurried from tree to tree and in among the brush. Sunlight filtered down through the treetops as Billy and Rashnin hurried past the thick trunks of many great and ancient trees. Finally Rashnin stopped in front of a massive tree; the trunk as wide as the shed in Billy's backyard!

Rashnin looked nervously around him and then whispered to Billy, "This is it. We must be certain no one sees us enter."

"Enter what?" Billy whispered back to him.

Rashnin stepped upon a rock by the base of the tree. To Billy's amazement, a hidden

< A Doorway Of Mirrors >   < By Katrina Mandrake-Johnston >   < 27 >

door in the side of the tree swung inwards. "Hurry," Rashnin told him, "before it closes."

Billy wondered if it were wise to have trusted Rashnin. He had mentioned that the man with no name had spies. Perhaps he had been one all along. Why had he been asking him such strange questions as he had?

Rashnin pushed Billy into the opening and followed close behind, as the door sealed after them. "I'm sorry, Billy, but we must hurry," Rashnin explained, "Follow me. I hope she is still here. It appears that this encampment has remained hidden since I was captured. I was worried that the man with no name might have discovered it during the time that I was imprisoned in the palace."

Billy followed Rashnin as he sped down a winding staircase down into the earth. He could see the large roots of the massive tree, here and there, as they descended. The stairs led to a huge cavern down inside the earth, and as Billy neared the bottom of the staircase, Billy saw that there were little houses here as well as a few shops. There were people here and many animal-like beings among them.

"We've made it," Rashnin announced, "We should be safe here. Come on, I will try to find her."

"But who are you talking about?" Billy wondered.

Rashnin added to his suspense by merely saying, "You will see."

CHAPTER 26

Billy was led to one of the shops. Inside the little building, he could see a few tables and chairs, numerous plants hanging from hooks on the walls giving the shop a tropical feel to it, and a back counter that was cluttered with small jars of various spices and dried herbs that Billy had never seen before.

"Queen Razzmeara, are you here? It's Rashnin. I have escaped the Ivory Palace and have brought someone with me. He is actually the one who freed me."

A very unusual being stepped gracefully from out of the shadows toward them. Billy couldn't help but stare in total amazement. It was a beautiful young woman, appearing not much older than his mother, wearing what looked to be a black feathered cloak about her. Her skin had a bluish tint to it, and instead of hair flowing about her face, long feathers like that of a peacock fell around her shoulders.

"Ah Rashnin, it is so good to see you again," she said speaking slowly and in a calm and soothing voice, "I am very surprised to see your guest, Rashnin."

"My name's Billy," he told her, "I like your feathered cloak."

"Oh dear me, child," she smiled at him, "This is not a cloak. These are my very own feathers; they are a part of me. Come, both of you, and sit here at this table. I shall make you some tea. And dear Rashnin, do not call me queen, as that was long ago."

Billy sat at one of the tables on a rickety wooden chair, and Rashnin, who could never sit upon a chair no matter how hard he tried, calmly waited for Razzmeara to return.

< A Doorway Of Mirrors >   < By Katrina Mandrake-Johnston >   < 28 >

"Rashnin?" Billy asked him, "What kind of place is this?"

"Yes, I guess we are able to relax now that we are here. We are in the encampment I spoke of. It once was home to a race of people who traveled within the underground. They tamed giant beetles and rode them through the vast maze of tunnels that connects to so many different places above. Now the entire race has disappeared. No one knows what happened to them either. When the man with no name came, many of us took refuge here," he explained, "After several years, even Queen Razzmeara was forced to go into hiding after being driven from her Ivory Palace. I fear the man with no name shall rule over everything and everyone very soon."

Razzmeara, holding a tray with three large steaming cups of tea, stepped nimbly from behind the counter and brought the tea to their table. Billy now saw this strange being's legs. They were covered in short brown fur like that of a deer. Her feet appeared human, but she had the sharp nails of an animal. As Razzmeara set the tray down on the table, Billy realized that her arms, from her shoulders down to her wrists, had silvery grey scales almost like a fish. Her hands were human, but still had the bluish tint to her skin that her face had.

She passed out the cups to the two of them and also placed one there for herself. Razzmeara put the tray up onto the counter and then pulled a chair over to join them. "Go ahead, it is alright," she said to Billy, "I think you will like it. It may smell a bit odd to you, but I assure you that it is quite delicious."

Rashnin put his little paws up onto the table, slurped up his tea in a matter of seconds, and then he dropped back down to the floor.

"Oh, please, Rashnin, do not let us keep you," she told him, "I am sure you have many friends you would like to revisit. I should warn you that quite a few have been taken since you were last here. It is good to see you well, dear Rashnin."

"Thank-you for the tea," he said, before speeding off out of the shop.

"Billy, do not look so worried. You are safe here," Razzmeara told him.

He was feeling quite nervous now that Rashnin had left them. He sipped at the tea and found it to have a fruity taste to it. He tried not to stare at her, as he didn't want to hurt her feelings. Weren't there supposed to be special rules of behavior around a queen? Billy didn't know what to do, so he just stared into his cup and took a few sips now and then.

"Oh dear," she exclaimed, "Could it be that I am the one who is making you so nervous? I realize that I must seem very odd compared to what you are used to. I see I must approach things slowly and carefully then."

She tapped a rhythm on the tabletop with her blue nails, as she tried to think of something to say. Billy's mom often did the same thing.

"Why don't you tell me a bit about your family?" she asked him, "Your mother, how is she?"

Billy decided if he were going to trust someone, it might as well be the queen. "My mom, she was the one that sent me here, through a mirror that brought me into the Ivory Palace. I never imagined that she would know about a place like this. She even had a magic mirror that allowed her to see into this world."

"Did you know that she grew up here? Well, until the man with no name came. It was far too dangerous for her then. Your grandfather took her with him back into his own world for her safety," Razzmeara explained.

"Really?" Billy said in amazement.

"Oh yes. You see, if the man with no name ever got a hold of her, he would surely have power over all of us," she told him.

< A Doorway Of Mirrors > < By Katrina Mandrake-Johnston >   < 29 >

"There are imposters of both me and my sister back in the other world. What if they push her through one of the mirrors?" Billy asked her with worry.

"The only mirror that can act as a gateway is the one that the grandfather clock has chosen to activate. Remember that it is only because you have the key that you are able to create a portal through other ones. Never lose that key, or both our worlds will be doomed," Razzmeara warned him.

"The imposter of me smashed my mom's magic mirror. She won't be able to help me anymore, and she must be so worried not knowing what is happening to me," Billy told her with tears starting in his eyes.

"Ah, yes, I used to have a mirror that allowed me to see into your world. Mine too was destroyed. I had to shatter it to keep it from falling into the hands of the man with no name. You see, he has tired of this world and is already looking for yet another to take over. He has already succeeded within your world more than you know. You and your sister are not the only imposters roaming about," she explained, "Oh and do not worry about your mother. She knows to be wary of them. If anything, she will be trying her best to keep them from trapping others here. I have a feeling she will not allow any friends over from school. I hope that will be enough though. They may begin to find her out."

"My grandfather passed away, but it turns out that he was an imposter as well. My mom brought home a book with the key inside, and there was a note from my real grandfather that said he tried to rescue the people here but probably got caught as well. So he is somewhere in this world. He must have been trapped here for several years. Do you think he's okay?" Billy asked her, "And my sister? The man with no name probably turned her into a slave, didn't he?"

Razzmeara bolted up from her chair. "What did you say?" she asked with an incredibly worried expression on her face, "John? He is here? I told him to stay away!"

"You knew my grandfather?" Billy asked her timidly.

"Oh, I am sorry," she said sitting back down, "I did not mean to frighten you. I am sure that he is all right. You see, dear, I have been putting this off, as I do not really know how to tell you this. I am much older than I appear. In fact, I am three hundred and twenty-nine years old."

"Wow!" Billy exclaimed, "I…"

She put up her hand to silence him. "I am sure Rashnin must have asked you about this or he would have never brought you to see me. You see, the reason why there are no photographs of your grandmother is because things from this world cannot be taken into the other."

"Yeah, Click was just a rock when I brought him back with me," he told her pulling him out to show her.

"I am glad that you have found this little one," she said giving Billy a warm smile, "He will be a big help to you. I am sure your mother must have brought back items from your grandfather's that had extraordinary powers when brought into this world, did she not? Do not let these fall into the hands of the man with no name. It was for this very reason that they were taken from this world. So have you figured out why there are no photographs of your grandmother?"

"She's from this world, isn't she?" said Billy.

"Yes, and although she could not return with your mother and grandfather, she watched on through her mirror. She was always there. Wherever there was a mirror in your world, she was there watching over her family. She watched you and Jenny grow up as well

< A Doorway Of Mirrors >   < By Katrina Mandrake-Johnston >   < 30 >

through the mirrors, until she was forced to destroy the magical one on this side."

"Wait a minute," Billy said starting to realize, "It's you, isn't it? You know my sister's name. All those things you know... it's you, isn't it? You were the one who had the magic mirror! You're my grandmother!"

"Yes, I am," she grinned, "Do you see why I was so reluctant to tell you this right away? You were so shocked by my appearance. To have told you that as well, so soon, would have overwhelmed you."

"I can't believe it!" he exclaimed.

"It is true. Go ahead, ask your little friend there," she suggested.

"Is Razzmeara my grandmother?" Billy asked Click.

"Buzz click click," he answered.

"It is true! So my mom is the princess," realized Billy, "and that's why the man with no name wants to capture her most of all?"

"Yes, the man with no name cannot hurt me, but if he ever captured her, the remaining people of this world would surrender to get her back unharmed," she told him, "I am thankful that Jenny knew nothing of all this. It means she will be safe. There may be a chance of restoring her, if she is indeed a slave now. Squeeshna is working on the task of finding a method of restoring slaves to normal."

"Oh, I met her," Billy told her, "The man with no name almost got her, but I saved her."

"Well done!" she beamed, "You have had quite an adventure it seems. Why don't I show you to the guest room? My home is attached to the back of the shop. You should get some rest."

"Grandma?" Billy said, trying to get used to the sound of it, "Click said that there was someone else in the Ivory Palace. Someone that smashed a bottle of something."

"Oh really? You know about that? Tomorrow then. Tomorrow, I shall tell you more about this. There may be hope for our world yet."

<< *** >> Next... - Return To The Ivory Palace <<***>>
****

About the author
       Writing stories, starting as young as seven, I've always been a big fan of fantasy, sci-fi, adventure, and horror, enjoying movies, comics, books, and video games with good story backgrounds.
       Writing has always been my passion. As a young writer, I found that I was bursting with ideas, always writing beginnings of stories, scenes and situations, or even just character personalities and backgrounds.
       Shortly after the completion of my first book at twenty-seven,
"World of Zaylyn - #1 - Quest For The Sword Of Anthrowst", my children suggested I start on a children's series as well. So, constantly writing, switching back and forth from the second book in the "World of Zaylyn" series to the "Doorway of Mirrors" children's series, it's been great fun.
       With the children's series, I went back to the writing style I had when I was younger, going over several of my story bits from seven to ten years old, to get the right feel for what I found exciting at that age and how a story develops in the mind of a child.
       I feel reading is very important for the development of a child's mind and imagination, as I know it had a large influence on me as a child. I hope to write many more books within the children's series and hope that my books will inspire the joy of reading in others, whether it be for the mere enjoyment of it or for educational purposes.
****

Special Thanks: To my two children who have shown incredible enthusiasm and support in my writing.
****

< A Doorway Of Mirrors >   < By Katrina Mandrake-Johnston >   < 31 >

<**> What has Billy learnt in his adventure?

Ch. 1 * Even if siblings don't always get along, deep down, they really love each other.
        * Never joke about serious things, as the fear remains even if it is untrue, and when something serious really does happen, because the trust has been damaged, you may not be believed which will make the serious event even worse.
Ch. 2 * If you can prepare for something, you should, and always take precautions, as you never know what may happen.
Ch. 3 * Always be wary of strangers, especially if you are alone.
        * If you do speak to a stranger, be sure to keep your distance and never ever get close enough for a stranger to grab hold of you.
        * Always trust your instincts. If something feels wrong, most likely it is.
        * With strangers, you never know what their true intentions are. Even if someone seems kind and trustworthy on the outside, they may not be on the inside.

Ch. 14 * Keeping someone around, faking a friendship, all because you want something from them or because they are of some use to you, is not friendship. It is a cruel and selfish way to treat someone.
        (You would never want to realize this about the people that you call friends and you should never do this to others. If you treat someone nicely to their face and are mean to them behind their back, this is a terrible thing to do. I am sad to say that, this happens very often. It is very damaging to a person's self-esteem, their sense of friendship and generosity, their ability to trust others, and it can make someone afraid to make new friends at all after being betrayed so horribly by this kind of bullying. If this happens to you, be aware of the damaging effect it can have on yourself and realize that it is the bully that is losing out on your friendship and not the other way around. Don't let it ruin who you are, because of a bully's silly opinion.)

Ch. 15 * You can always make a difference, no matter how small. With everyone doing their small part, a large goal can be met.
Ch. 16 * Always think of the consequences of your actions and whether others will be affected by it.
Ch. 17 * Sometimes, when you think your parents can't possibly understand what's going on in your life, you discover that they sometimes have a much better understanding than you have about certain things and that they are able to help you when it seemed no one could.
        * Sometimes a parent has to trust in their children to make decisions on their own in their own life adventures. It is very hard for a parent to give a child this freedom of independence, and you should never abuse this trust and always do what you know to be the right thing to do.

Ch. 26 * Just because family and friends can longer be with you in body, know that they will always watch over you and be with you in spirit. You are never truly alone in anything.

* Things are not always as they appear.
* When things look hopeless, you should never give up. If you do that, then things really will be.
* Always try to learn as much information as you are able, as information is a very powerful tool and vital for understanding the world around you.
* Have faith in yourself and your decisions. If you do make a mistake, accept it and most importantly try to learn from it.

<**> What other things do you think Billy has learnt in his adventure?

****

A DOORWAY OF MIRRORS

Return To The Ivory Palace

<A Doorway Of Mirrors><Return To The Ivory Palace> < By Katrina Mandrake-Johnston > < 1 >

CHAPTER 1

Billy awoke to the darkness of the room. His mind wandered back to his amazing

dream... how his sister, Jenny, had been replaced by a strange duplicate… how he had discovered the mysterious portal through the mirror in Jenny's room that was somehow connected to the old grandfather clock. He had dreamt that his grandfather was still alive and trapped along with Jenny in this other world that lay beyond through the mirrors.

He had met the man with no name whom has been enslaving the people and creatures of this world to do as he pleases. Billy shuddered as he remembered how that evil man had lashed out towards him with his squid-like hand and how one of his tentacle fingers had stung his cheek with its touch.

A duplicate of Billy was now lurking about, trying to take his place, but his mother had known. She had helped him as best as she could and had watched him through her magic mirror as he had struggled through that strange place, until the imposter Billy had smashed it to pieces.

He remembered the talking clock he had spoken to in the grey and dusty shop. Click, the little disk-like being, had helped him through the metal tunnels to escape the prickly creature that had been chasing him down. Billy shuddered again. That creature would have surely killed him, and he was lucky Squeeshna had found him and had been able to treat him for the poison spines it had struck his legs with.

Billy lay awake in the darkness, thankful it had only been a dream. "*It is awfully dark,*" he thought to himself, noticing again that the blankets and mattress had a different feel to them. "*Of course it was a dream,*" he said to himself, "*Something like that can't possibly be real.*"

Squeeshna had been some sort of lemur, although much larger, nearly his own size, and if it weren't for her looking like a fuzzy animal, he would have been sure he had been talking to a proper person. She had been trying to find a way to restore her brother, as he too had his essence drained and crystallized by the man with no name. She had her brother's crystal but was struggling to find a way to restore him back to normal. Billy had helped her to get the herbs she needed to continue her study into the crystals and how to restore a person's essence back into the body. The man with no name would

<A Doorway Of Mirrors><Return To The Ivory Palace> < By Katrina Mandrake-Johnston > < ? >

have captured her if Billy had not distracted him. Billy was instead captured and imprisoned in the Ivory Palace.

Luckily, he was able to use the mysterious key his grandfather had left behind and was able to escape back to his home world through a mirror there. The man with no name didn't seem to know that the mirrors were linked to Billy's ability to travel back and forth between the worlds, which was something Billy had to be very

careful about. He had even found a note his grandfather had left behind in the Ivory Palace which gave clues to magical objects Billy could bring across to aid him in his journey.

Billy freed a large hedgehog creature named Rashnin whom had been imprisoned within the Ivory Palace, and together they escaped from a horrible creature lurking within the palace walls that had the body of a serpent, the talons of a bird of prey, and the large head of a crocodile. Rashnin took Billy to a secret underground encampment where most of the people still free of the man with no name kept hidden from him and his spies.

There,
Billy was

introduced to an odd-looking woman that used to be their queen before the man with no name took over the land for his own. Her name was Razzmeara. Her skin was a faint blue color and black feathers fell about her shoulders like a cloak although they were her own. Instead of hair upon her head, long feathers like that of a peacock draped about her face and shoulders. Her legs were covered in short brown fur like that of a deer and her feet had the long claw-like nails of an animal. Razzmeara's arms, from her shoulders down to her wrists, had silvery grey scales almost like a fish. Her face and hands

appeared human, despite the bluish tint to her skin, and even though she was over three hundred years old, she looked not much older than his mother. What was most odd about his dream, Billy decided, was that Razzmeara was supposed to be his grandmother.

"It had only been a dream, right?" Billy asked himself.

<A Doorway Of Mirrors><Return To The Ivory Palace> < By Katrina Mandrake-Johnston > < 3 >

"Billy?" a woman's voice called out, "Are you awake? I have prepared a bit of breakfast for you. There are quite a few things I would like to discuss with you concerning our world."

"Yes, Razzmeara... I mean, Grandma," Billy called out, realizing that no matter how dream-like all that was happening seemed to be, that it was real. Jenny and his grandfather needed his help in order for them to be rescued, as did so many others from this world.

CHAPTER 2

Razzmeara came through the doorway into the bedroom carrying a lantern which she placed upon a small wooden table. She gave Billy a warm smile and departed back into the other room. The wondrous and exotic smell of what he hoped was to be his breakfast came wafting into his room and made his mouth water. Billy dressed and carried the lantern through into the other room.

"The light will not start to filter down from above until it nears high noon," Razzmeara explained, "Come and sit beside me here at the table, dear. I have prepared quite a few favorites of your mother's for you this morning. I am sure you will enjoy them just as she did as a child."

Billy sat at the table, set the lantern down at the edge of the table, and stared at the plate of strange food items. One yellowy and slippery-looking lump reminded Billy of a large slug he had once seen. Another piece looked like a dark purple cotton ball with countless spidery legs sticking out of it. There were long pink tube-like pieces that Billy decided might be some sort of worm. A cup of thick lime green goo was beside the plate. Billy shook his head, his hunger fading very quickly at the sight of these things.

"I know this might look quite different compared to what you are used to, Billy, but it is quite delicious. You should at least try it," she told him.

Billy poked at the wiggly yellow blob on his plate. It was disgusting. It was slimy and sticky. He shut his eyes tight, and already making a terrible face at his so-called breakfast, he dared to taste the little that had gotten on his finger. He opened his eyes wide in surprise and a smile spread across his lips.

"It tastes like custard, well, almost," said Billy, and he picked up the cup of slimy liquid to try a taste. He was pleasantly surprised at the wonderful taste this had as well. "This tastes almost like a mixture of honeydew melon and strawberries," he said with delight.

"Go on, try the other two," Razzmeara said with a smile.

Billy couldn't decide whether the pink tube pieces tasted more like deep-fried prawns or bacon, and the spidery purple puff had the flavor of what Billy suspected a marshmallow dipped in grape jelly to have.

"Now Billy," said Razzmeara, taking on a serious tone, "You said that you came across a room filled with various bottles and that you believe someone to still be imprisoned there in the Ivory Palace?"

"Yes, Click was certain of that," Billy explained and remembered how the effort made to gain that answer had almost cost poor Click his life.

"My magician, Nemfootoe, who dabbled mostly into potions, was captured by the man with no name some time ago. I feared that he may have been changed into one of his slaves, but perhaps not. You see, he bravely offered to enter the palace in order to spy on what the man with no name might be up to. My magician escaped with the rest of us some time after his laboratory was destroyed and his existing potions were stolen. He used an invisibility potion, that he had saved, to enter the palace undetected. What I believe to have happened now is that he found the room where his potions were being stored and he was attempting to mix another invisibility potion when he was discovered. Perhaps he was the one that smashed the bottle upon the floor that you found. He may have done so to keep the formula from the man with no name. That information would doom us all if he were to discover it. Nemfootoe said that the potion he had used would not last very long, so I am assuming that this is what happened. It seems the man with no name is merely collecting up anything he feels may pose a threat to him, as he must not be putting the potions to use by what you have told me. It appears he is merely storing them away in order to keep them from those that have escaped his grip. I believe he was doing the same with the herbs Squeeshna was after. My magician, he left some of the potion behind with me for safe keeping. Billy, if you truly think you are able to return to the Ivory Palace and rescue him, I shall give it to you. You must understand, however, that this task will be very dangerous. But, if you are able to succeed where he had failed, it could prove very useful to us all."

"Yes," said Billy bravely, "I want to try to rescue him, and I'll try to find out any information I can that might help us against the man with no name."

CHAPTER 3

"Very well," replied Razzmeara, "I shall retrieve the potion for you then. Can you remember the way back to the Ivory Palace from here?"

"I think so," answered Billy, a little unsure of himself and of what he had just offered to do.

She got up from the table, and taking the lantern, she placed it upon the countertop of the shop. Razzmeara began to rummage around behind the counter as she searched for the bottle. "You should wait until you are about to enter, as the effects will not last very long unfortunately," she warned him.

"Yes, I understand," he told her nervously, "Maybe someone could go with me," he suggested.

"You would be detected for sure. It is safer if you go alone. And..." she said hesitating, "I cannot be sure of whom I can fully trust. The man with no name has many spies. He has his slaves, yes, but also he has made many promises that have twisted people into betrayal. Even Rashnin I cannot bring myself to completely trust, which frightens me as he has become one of my most loyal friends."

"How can you be sure that I am not one of his spies then? What if I am a duplicate of the real Billy like what he sent into my world to fool my mom?" asked Billy.

"I would be suspicious if you had been anyone else," she answered, bringing the lantern and a small bottle with her over to the table, "Since you have knowledge of the other world, your home world, I know that you are true."

"Oh, I see," said Billy, "So this is the potion?"

She handed him the bottle. It was rounded at the bottom with a narrow neck. A brown cork was jammed tightly into the neck of the bottle to hold it closed and the glass was a

<A Doorway Of Mirrors><Return To The Ivory Palace> < By Katrina Mandrake-Johnston > < 5 >

dark blue. Billy shook the tiny bottle and could hear that there was only a small amount of liquid swishing about in the bottom.

"I'm sorry that there is not more in there for you, Billy," she told him sadly, "You will be invisible to your own eyes as well which may be a little alarming at first and will take some getting used to. You should begin your journey soon. I will walk with you to the top of the staircase to the hidden entrance." She picked up the lantern once more to bring with them.

"How will I find my way back?" Billy asked, getting up from the table and walking with his grandmother to the door of the shop to leave.

"Yes, the entrance is well hidden; you may well have difficulty finding it again. I shall send my scouts to guide you upon your return. Simply look to the birds. They will show you the way," she told him with a smile, "Billy, it would not be wise to call me Grandmother so openly. Remember why your mother had to flee to the safety of your world. The man with no name might try to use that connection against me and the people here. As I am the queen, your mother is a princess of this world and so are you in turn a prince. Any spies that may be lurking about may have already grown curious about why I have been speaking to you in such great lengths."

"I understand. I will be careful," he assured her.

She nodded and opened the door to the shop. Razzmeara then led him through the encampment by the light of the lantern to the staircase that spiraled up to the surface. It didn't seem that anyone else was awake yet, as he couldn't see any other lights within the buildings or anyone else out and about as they walked.

Perhaps he was wrong. *"Could there really be spies here as well?"* Billy wondered, *"Rashnin had seemed to think that this was the one place where we were safe. I can't see how anyone could willingly side with the man with no name. But I guess, if he offers them money or something. No wait, I bet he tells them lies about freeing their family and friends from being slaves if they help him. If they think helping that evil man is the only way they can save the people they love… I guess I really do have to be careful about whom I trust, but that doesn't mean I'm not going to try my best to help the people I come across. If I thought like that, I would have been too afraid to help Rashnin out of the Ivory Palace and, therefore, probably wouldn't have made it out alive or found this place and the grandmother I didn't even know I had."*

"Razzmeara?" Billy asked.

"Yes, Billy?" she said, as the long animal claws of her blue feet clicked against the stairs as they climbed.

"Do you think my mom is okay? I'm really worried about her and my dad too. What if they try to push my dad into the mirror in Jenny's room? As soon as the grandfather clock chimes, the gateway will open," he said watching the black feathers ruffle about her shoulders and back and the light from the lantern gleam off the silvery fish-like scales of her arms.

"I am certain that she will do her best to keep that from happening, but if it does, our efforts to stop the man with no name and restore those he has enslaved must continue even if your mother is captured as well. If your father falls into this world, your mother will surely follow having all of her family trapped here on this side. The only reason she has not come after you and Jenny is to keep your father safe from the imposters there. She knows of the danger here and that the man with no name will try his hardest to capture her most of all, but her love for her family will outweigh that danger. So many have lost hope already and her capture will surely cause many more to give up completely. We must all remain strong and fight back no matter what." Razzmeara came to stop at the door at the top of the stairs.

<A Doorway Of Mirrors><Return To The Ivory Palace> < By Katrina Mandrake-Johnston > < 6 >

She placed her light blue hand affectionately to Billy's cheek, the dark blue color of her nails sparkling in the lantern light. "You shall be my valiant knight, Billy. I hate to send you into such a danger, to place such responsibility upon you so soon, but you are our only hope. You are the one thing the man with no name wasn't expecting; the one thing he is unsure about in his plans."

"I will try my best," Billy said in a shaky voice.

"Oh, you are so brave," Razzmeara said with tears in her eyes and she hugged him gently. The long peacock feathers that were in place of her hair tickled his nose as they brushed against his face.

She kissed him on the forehead and then went over to open the door to the forest beyond.

CHAPTER 4

Billy stepped out into the sunshine that filtered down through the treetops far above him. Razzmeara had closed the secret door and now it appeared as if Billy were merely standing in front of an enormous tree. He examined the bark, and even though he knew the door to be there, he could not find the seams that would indicate where it was. He would never be able to find it again when he returned. If for some reason Razzmeara were unable to send the birds she spoke of to guide him, he would definitely become hopelessly lost.

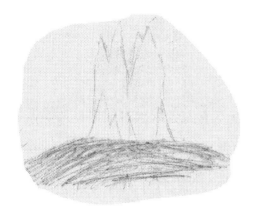

Billy walked among the trees, enjoying the sunlight that shone down on him. The air was cool and refreshing.

He walked until he came to the forest's edge, and he looked across the grassy fields and up to where the Ivory Palace stood like a large jagged tooth sticking up out of the ground.

He made his way toward it, all the while keeping a watchful eye out for any sign of danger. Everything was calm and peaceful.

Eventually, Billy came to stand at the oval shaped door. This was the door that he and Rashnin had discovered. It was disguised to look like a large mirror on the wall. If they hadn't felt the draft seeping into the room from around the mirror's edge, they wouldn't have known that it was a way out for them. The door was slightly ajar. Billy hoped that this was simply because it hadn't closed all the way after he and Rashnin had gone through it the first time. He wondered if they had been seen in their escape and if the creature had laid a trap for anyone returning this way.

Billy felt around in his pocket and retrieved the tiny blue bottle. He took hold of the cork and wiggled it back and forth until it came free of the bottle with a loud pop. Billy immediately held it away from him as the liquid inside had a horrible, awful smell to it. "Yuck! It stinks so bad! I'm supposed to drink this disguising thing?!" Billy remarked to himself, but he held his nose and gulped it down. It tasted like chalk and tuna fish. It smelt

<A Doorway Of Mirrors><Return To The Ivory Palace> < By Katrina Mandrake-Johnston > < 7 >
worse than it tasted. He put the cork back into the empty bottle and placed it back into his pocket once more.

When he brought his hand out again, it was gone. His hand had vanished completely. He stared in disbelief. "It's working!" Billy exclaimed in amazement, "I'm really turning invisible!"

Billy watched himself slowly disappear. He was relieved to see that his clothing also was effected by the magic of the potion. He was extremely thankful that he wouldn't have to be running around naked.

He went to open the door and it took him quite awhile just to grab hold of it. He couldn't see his hand, although he knew it was there, so he had to find the door more by a sense of touch. He finally ended up waving his arm about until he felt the cool surface of the door and then had to slide his hand down to find where the opening was. Billy then pulled open the door just enough to be able to squeeze through. He didn't want to make it too

obvious that the door was opening. To anyone that might be watching, he wanted it to look like it had been only a strong breeze that had moved the door.

Once inside, Billy could see the massive stone dragon in the corner of the room where he and Rashnin had hidden behind when the reptilian creature was searching for them. Razzmeara had said that this dragon had been alive and a protector of the Ivory Palace when she had ruled here. The man with no name had somehow turned him to stone and had therefore been able to drive Razzmeara from her palace, as without the dragon, she could not stand against the man with no name and his growing army of slaves.

"*It must have been terrible,*" thought Billy, "*She had no choice but to hand over the Ivory Palace to the man with no name. If she had given the command to fight back, it would only mean that the innocent people the man with no name had enslaved would be the ones getting hurt. I wonder what the dragon could have done? Perhaps the people, even under his evil control, would have been too afraid to approach with the dragon on guard, or maybe the dragon held some sort of power that could be used against the man with no name.*"

Billy listened at the door to the hallways for the sound the reptilian creature made as it side-winded through the passageways. He heard nothing; all was clear. Even though Billy was invisible, he didn't want to come across that beast if he could help it. Billy awkwardly felt around in his pocket for the round piece of glass that allowed him to see past the illusion hiding the doors and side passageways of the halls beyond. He took it from his pocket, and holding it up to his eye, he opened the door and stepped into the hallway.

CHAPTER 5

Billy walked quietly down the hall until he came to the nearest junction. He looked to the right, down the passageway, to where he could see the two doors. One had been where Rashnin had been imprisoned and the other was where the bottles were being stored. "*Too bad I don't know the formula to make another invisibility potion. If I'm going to do anything here I'll have to do it quickly before the potion wears off,*" Billy thought nervously.

Billy looked ahead of him to where the reptilian creature had come from when he and Rashnin had been trying to escape. There was another passageway to his left as well. Billy

<A Doorway Of Mirrors><Return To The Ivory Palace> < By Katrina Mandrake Johnston > < 8 >
wondered if he should ask Click which would be the best way to go. Would the creature be drawn to Click's buzzes and clicking sounds? Would the creature be able to sense that Billy was there, even when he was invisible? Billy couldn't afford to go down the wrong hallway. If the potion wore off before he found the magician or before he could snoop around and escape again, he would be in terrible danger. If he could find the magician, maybe Billy could return to the bottle room in time to make another potion. If he succeeded, then both of them could escape completely unseen.

Billy reached into his pocket and felt around for Click. He pulled him out and held his little friend in front of him. As Billy stared into the nothing before him, he whispered, "Click? It's me. We're both invisible and we're back in the Ivory Palace. We need to find the queen's magician, Nemfootoe, and quickly before the potion wears off. Can you tell me which way to go?"

"Buzz click click," he answered and the sound echoed down the smooth white passageways.

"Okay, so yes, you can," said Billy. He was worried about asking him anything that might be too difficult for him. "Should I go to the right to find him?" asked Billy.

"Buzz buzz," said Click.

"Oh great, so then that means I should go straight and that's just where the creature had come from last time I was here," Billy said in a whisper, "This is going to be very dangerous, isn't it?"

"Buzz click click," he answered, meaning yes.

Billy carefully placed Click back into his pocket and headed down the hallway, still holding the glass piece up before him. He walked until he came to another junction. He took Click out of his pocket once more and asked him again which way to go. Click gave him his answer, and Billy followed his instructions at each junction they came to.

Finally, Billy and Click arrived at a narrow staircase that led to an upper floor. So far there had been no sign of the reptilian creature which Billy was thankful for. He had no idea of how much longer the potion would last, but he hoped it would be long enough to find Nemfootoe and get back out of the palace again. Billy went up the stairs and came to yet another hallway. At the far end, there was a large wooden door with a small barred window near the top. Quite a ways before the door, however, there was a large opening in the left wall of the passageway. Billy lowered the glass piece and discovered that he no longer needed it in this part of the palace. He put it into his pocket with the empty bottle, Click, and the two strange marbles from out of the cat statues.

He was still invisible, but he was still nervous of passing by the opening. Billy could hear the sound of water and could see a bit of the leafy vegetation that covered the floor of the room beyond. Could this be where the reptilian creature lived? The door at the end of the passageway must be where Nemfootoe was being held captive. If he crept past all the way to the door and called out to the prisoner, would the creature come after him and start stabbing around with his spear trying to find where Billy was?

He decided that he had to at least go to the window and see if anyone was inside. He would have a lot more to worry about if the potion ran out on him. His only chance was to somehow find out the formula and make another potion from the room with all the bottles and do all of that before this one wore off.

Billy made his way along the passage and looked through the large opening into the room. The floor of the small room was covered in leafy vines, and at the back, a large fountain bubbled water out of numerous spouts to splash into the wide basin below. There also seemed

<A Doorway Of Mirrors><Return To The Ivory Palace> < By Katrina Mandrake-Johnston > < 9 >

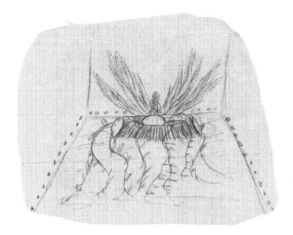

to be jets positioned along the bottom of the walls that would send a fine spray out and over the floor every couple of seconds. The mist that it created rolled out over the leaves of the vines, clouding the floor from view. In the center of the fountain, its roots twisting and hugging the stone of the center piece and the basin surrounding it, was an enormous plant. It appeared that the vines were connected to this center plant and that all the vegetation in the room was part of this single plant. The giant, long fern-like leafs around the fountain extended up from the bulk of this unusual plant, and Billy could see that there was a large round and yellowy egg-like object sitting in the water of the basin that appeared to be the main root from which everything had grown. Except for the fountain and the plant, the room was empty. If this were indeed the lair of the reptilian creature, it was not in here right now.

Billy continued to the door at the end of the hall. He peered into the room through the small barred window and saw a skinny man in dark blue robes sitting on a cot in the corner of the room. He had wispy grey hair, and he was simply staring sadly in front of him, seemingly lost in thought.

"Hey," Billy whispered, "Are you Nemfootoe?"

CHAPTER   6

"I've come to help," Billy told the man, "Can you hear me?"

The man merely continued to sit, staring blankly at the wall. He appeared to be in some sort of trance. Billy wondered if Nemfootoe had maybe been turned into a slave, but he also wondered why he had been imprisoned if he were already under the control of the man with no name. A fear came over Billy now as he considered that perhaps it was a trap. He looked nervously around, grateful that the potion was still working to keep him hidden.

If the door were unlocked, Billy would be sure that it was some sort of trap. If not, he didn't know what to think. Billy bravely tried the handle and found it to be locked. Would the man with no name lock up one of his slaves? *"The man inside seems to be nothing but an empty shell. He's just staring off into nothingness. Could it be that he's in some sort of magical trance?"* Billy wondered.

"Hey! Hello in there!" Billy whispered a little louder, as he tried to get the man's attention, "You're Nemfootoe the queen's magician, right? I'm here to free you. Are you all right?"

The man made no sign that he had heard him. Billy let out a frustrated sigh. The potion probably wouldn't last much longer, and it seemed that Nemfootoe was in no shape to be rescued or fit to tell him how to mix a new potion. He would have to return to Razzmeara empty-handed, and the potion she had given him would have been completely wasted when it could have been put to good use in some other task. *"At least she will know what has happened to Nemfootoe and that there is no hope of using his knowledge of magical mixtures against the man with no name,"* Billy tried to convince himself, *"At least there is something I*

<A Doorway Of Mirrors><Return To The Ivory Palace> < By Katrina Mandrake Johnston >< 10 >
can tell her as a result of me coming back here."

As he moved away from the door to return to the stairs, he heard a voice call out. Billy spun around, hoping that it had been Nemfootoe. Had it come from behind the door? Billy wasn't quite sure about that.

"Do come closer," the voice repeated, a little clearer now. Billy was sure that it had not come from behind the door; the voice was coming from somewhere inside the room with the vegetation. Perhaps it was another talking animal like Squeeshna and Rashnin.

Billy was nervous and was glad for his invisibility. Whoever it was that had spoken must have only heard him. He hoped to get a good look at whomever it was in the room before he did anything. He quietly approached the opening and stepped into the room. Mist swirled about his feet but did not give him away. He had to be careful not to rustle the leafy vines laying around him, however, as to bump them as he moved would definitely show that he was there. He scanned the room but saw nothing except for the plant and the fountain. Billy suspected that whomever it was might be hidden beneath the leaves or maybe even submerged under the water in the basin of the fountain.

"What is your name?" the voice asked.

"Billy," he answered, sure that he could not be seen. He didn't want to give up the chance that this could be someone that could help him. As long as he stayed cautious and the potion continued to last, he would be all right.

"That is quite an unusual name," the voice commented and then asked, "Did I hear you say that you were here to free the magician? What was it you called him? Nemfootoe?" The jets hissed the misty spray out over the floor again.

"I… I was hoping to, but something is wrong with him," answered Billy nervously, "He's just staring blankly at the wall."

"I know what has happened to him. Would you like me to tell you?" asked the voice.

"Yes, please," said Billy, as the jet released yet another spray across the floor.

"Do come closer into the room, child," coaxed the voice.

"No, it's all right," said Billy warily, "I can hear you just fine from where I am." Was the voice trying to trick him or did this person actually know what happened? Billy had a funny feeling inside that something wasn't quite right here. When he was little, his mom had warned him about strangers that might try to kidnap children; leading them away from their parents, pretending that they needed help with something, promising them candy or some sort of reward, and tricking them into getting into a car or even grabbing hold and forcing the child into a car where they could drive far away from anyone that could save them. It's frightening to think that someone could be as evil to do such a thing, but to know about it and to take precautions are the best methods for safety. Billy just had a bad feeling about this, and he needed to keep his distance and watch what exactly he said to this person just in case he were in danger.

"I can't quite get a good look at you, child, and I'm finding it a little hard to hear you too. Why don't you come into the room and sit down for awhile," suggested the voice. Another misty spray shot out from the jets again. The voice went on to say, "The man with no name, do you know him? I know exactly what happened to your poor friend Nemfootoe. I even stopped the man with no name from completing his plans with the magician, did you know that? He would have become a full slave, had I not interfered."

"Really?" Billy exclaimed with delight. Perhaps this was a friend after all; another person imprisoned here in the Ivory Palace. "So what happened? What did you do?" asked Billy.

<A Doorway Of Mirrors><Return To The Ivory Palace> < By Katrina Mandrake-Johnston >< 11 >

The jets hissed out another bout of mist to roll across the floor. This time, Billy wasn't completely certain if it had just been the spray that had rustled the leaves or if something else had. Perhaps something had been timing its movements with the spray from the jets. Billy was still invisible, but he thought that maybe he should move away and out into the hall. *"What about the sound of my footsteps?"* Billy wondered. He decided to stay where he was instead. If anything approached out of the leaves and the mist, he would be able to see it and escape because of his invisibility. Anything or anyone would think that he was hiding from view somewhere in the hallway, not watching from a few feet inside the room where he was.

"I stole away the crystal," answered the voice plainly, "One of the servants was taking it to the man with no name. Once he had possession of Nemfootoe's crystal, he would have been able to manipulate his body like a puppet, maybe even fool the queen into letting her guard down around the enslaved magician. I have been here in the Ivory Palace a long time, and I could not let the man with no name defeat Razzmeara like that. So Nemfootoe sits there empty. Not himself, but not under the control of the man with no name either." The mist rolled out across the floor and over the vegetation once more from the jets.

"Well, I am glad of that then, thank-you," said Billy, "Is there anything else you could tell me that might help? Did the magician say anything to you before he was captured or anything like that? Or do you know anything that might help against the man with no name? And what about the crystals; do you know anything about them? Is it possible to restore someone that has been made into a slave?"

"Ah, so curious, so many questions all at once, so many things gone unanswered," sighed the voice, "He did not speak to me, no, and I do not have the answers you desire. I still have the crystal, however." The jets released another spray into the room. "Would you like it? You may take it with you if you like. It may help. It's just there, a little to the right of you, on the floor there. Do you see it?"

Billy looked over to the area beside him, and as the mist shifted about, he caught a glimpse of a yellowy-orange shard about the length of his hand. *"Wait a minute,"* Billy thought in fear, *"What did the voice just say? To the right of me? How does it know where I am? I'm still invisible. How does it know where I am?!"*

"No, I don't see it," Billy told the voice, hoping that he might be able to fool it into believing that he was somewhere out in the hall, "Would I have to come into the room to find it?" The jets hissed their release of spray once more and rustled the leaves again as they had done each time. Billy couldn't see anything hiding beneath the leaves from where he was, but he was afraid and even more afraid of moving from where he was for fear of making noise. Could it find him just by following the sound of his voice? If that were true, it couldn't be certain of exactly where he was.

"Oh, no, whatever you like," said the voice in a cheerful tone, "You can stay where you are if you feel comfortable there. I can clear away some of the vines for you if you'd like, if it makes it easier for you."

"Ah, okay," said Billy, not knowing what to think. Could he really trust this person? Had all this talk of spies clouded his judgment? Whoever this is clearly wants to help and had even stopped the man with no name from completing his plans with Nemfootoe. Perhaps this person was a friend of Razzmeara's after all and has remained hidden away in here all this time.

The vines began to move, but Billy still couldn't see anyone. *"Could it be someone invisible just as I am? Perhaps in this world there are beings that are naturally invisible. Maybe that is why this person can see me in this state as it is normal for them to see others that are invisible like them,*" thought Billy.

When the vines had cleared away, Billy stared in horror. There upon the floor were the bones and clothing of some poor unfortunate person. Beside one of the outstretched skeletal hands was the crystal. The vines were still moving, and Billy finally realized that it was not something hiding within the leafy vines, but instead, it was the plant itself that was after him.

The jets hissed out their misty spray, and Billy dashed forward and grabbed the crystal from the floor. A large vine, that had been creeping towards him all the time that he and the voice had been speaking, now lifted up from the floor. Billy could see the large thorny spikes along its length. It was like a snake-like barbed wire and it was ready to entangle him. His invisibility wasn't doing him any good here. This plant could either sense the vibrations of his voice or maybe even sense the heat of his body.

Billy ran frantically for the hallway as it lashed out at him. The vine wrapped tightly around his ankle and pulled him hard to the ground. The jets released their mist into the room again, and the vine began to drag him back into the room in short rapid jerks. If he were dragged far enough into the room where the other shorter vines could grab hold of him as well, he would never be able to escape.

After a few tugs and Billy had been pulled a little distance back into the room, the vine stopped, almost as if it were resting after taking such effort to pull Billy back in. Billy sat up and tried to yank and pull his leg free of the vine. It squeezed tighter and he screamed in pain as the thorns dug into the flesh of his ankle. The mist was sent out over the floor once again.

The vine began to pull again at Billy, and he continued to be slowly dragged along the ground farther and farther into the room. The floor was smooth and there was nothing Billy could grab on to. He was helpless. He tried to release the vine's hold by stabbing at it with the crystal, but it was much too tough and there wasn't enough time. There wasn't anything he could do to cut through the thick sinewy vine to free his leg.

After the plant had made a few short tugs on Billy's leg to bring him closer, the vine stopped again. "*Is it connected to the spray somehow? It only seems to move after the spray has come out to wet its leaves. I hope I'm right,*" thought Billy, and he lifted his entangled leg up and above the reach of the jets. The spray was sent out over the vines yet again, but this time, the vine that held him remained dry.

To Billy's relief, he was not pulled any farther. The vine's grip weakened, and Billy was able to free his leg. He now held the vine in his hand. Keeping the vine above the mist, Billy stood and threw the vine as far as he could across the room, hoping that it would give him enough time to escape before the plant could send it out again to grab hold of him. He ran quickly into the hall, noticing how much the plant's thorns had hurt his ankle.

"Where are you going?" the voice called out with a cruel laugh.

"So all you told me was a lie!" Billy called back to the plant.

"Oh, no, everything I told you was the truth," the plant explained, "Attacking the servant was not completely without purpose; not simply done out of hunger. I could not let the man with no name use Nemfootoe to defeat Razzmeara in some sort of deception. If anyone shall come to triumph over her, it will be me. You see, it was her that imprisoned me here long ago in her Ivory Palace." The jets released another bout of mist, but Billy was well clear of the plant's reach now. "The nutrients in this damn spray are simply enough to keep me alive and dormant," the plant went on to tell him, "When I lived in the swamps, I devoured people in great numbers and I was incredibly powerful. My budlings had spread out over the land, claiming the swamp for my own and then gradually the lands around it. Razzmeara eventually

<A Doorway Of Mirrors><Return To The Ivory Palace> < By Katrina Mandrake-Johnston >< 13 >
defeated me and kept me here where I could not find prey or send my budlings out into other areas."

"So you ate the servant that was carrying the crystal. Why didn't you escape then?" Billy asked in curiosity, as he nursed his invisible ankle.

"I had gained my strength then, my power, but there was no one to carry my budlings. Nemfootoe was but a useless husk that could do nothing but sit and stare lifelessly at the wall. I'm surprised he's still alive actually. I suppose in that trance-like state, it has reduced his body to almost a type of hibernation." Billy heard the rhythmic hiss of the jets once more. The plant continued, "I suppose you are to run back to your queen now? So go. There is nothing left for you here now. Watch out for the creature in the halls. I'd hate to think of you gobbled up and going to waste in that foul thing's belly."

Thankful that his invisibility was still lasting and might help to hide him from the reptilian creature and his deadly spear and jaws, Billy got up and headed down the stairs.

<u>CHAPTER 7</u>

Once downstairs again, Billy took the glass piece out of his pocket and had a look around. He had memorized which way he and Click had gone just in case he were unable to ask him how to get back again. All he had to do was do everything in reverse.

Billy looked at the yellowy-orange crystal shard that appeared to float in the air in front of him as he held it in his invisible hand. Just then, he felt an electric spark from within his pocket that gave him quite a jolt. Billy thought that there might be something wrong with Click, but when he put his hand into his pocket, he felt that the two marbles were the ones that had done it.

He held them out in front of him, but they too were invisible. Suddenly, what looked to be a lightening bolt shot out from where the marbles were in one hand and out to the crystal in his other.

Billy stared in amazement at what was happening. The crystal was now beginning to glow with a strange blue light. He was even more surprised when he heard a faint voice coming from the shard.

"What's going on?! Where am I?! It's me, Nemfootoe! Is anyone there?!" the voice from the crystal said in fear.

"Your essence has been trapped within a crystal by the man with no name and your body has been left in some sort of trance. You haven't been made into a slave yet though. I'm trying to help you, if I can," Billy told him quickly.

"Oh my. This is not good, not good at all," remarked Nemfootoe, "I suspect Razzmeara, our queen, has sent you into the Ivory Palace using what little of the invisibility potion we had left, am I right?"

"Yes, that's right," replied Billy, "Can you tell me how to make another one before this one wears off?"

"Yes, of course, but you must hurry," warned the magician, "Are you in the room with all the bottles?"

"No, but I can get there," answered Billy.

"Very well," said Nemfootoe, "I shall explain along the way."

Billy put the marbles back in his pocket and removed the glass piece so he could find his way back to the bottle room. Billy thought to himself, "*I sure look like one of those ghosts out of a movie with the crystal looking like it's floating along the passageway by itself, and even more so with this funny glow around it. I hope it lasts. Maybe the marbles can help to*

<A Doorway Of Mirrors><Return To The Ivory Palace> < By Katrina Mandrake Johnston >< 14 >

identify what crystal belongs to whom, but I don't think they will be able to build up a large enough charge to activate more than one. It might be days before they are recharged. I sure would like to know how they work. Razzmeara probably knows."

"First mix liquid from the triangular-shaped bottle that has green glass, purple liquid, and smells like Neefelb berries," Nemfootoe instructed.

"I don't know what those berries smell like or even what they are; I'm not from this world," Billy explained, as he rounded the corner at one of the junctions.

"Oh dear," exclaimed Nemfootoe, "This is not good, not good at all, as there are several bottles, and if you don't choose the right one by the smell, your potion could go horribly wrong. All I can tell you is that they have a sweet fragrance with just the hint of what, ah, I suppose similar to freshly cut grass."

"Okay, I'll try my best," Billy told him.

"You need to fill your container until it's about a fourth full from this bottle," instructed Nemfootoe. Billy came to another junction and continued down the correct hallway. "Second, you need to find a dark blue bottle with a square bottom and a neck that spirals up. It's an unusually shaped bottle so you won't have any trouble finding that one. Now you must be very careful only to put in three drops from this bottle... no more and no less," warned the magician, "Third, will be a short and wide oval-shaped bottle. You must fill your container now to reach almost to the top. Make sure there is roughly an eighth left for the last ingredient. This liquid in the oval bottle will be a milky white and will smell like Randosh mushrooms. Do not confuse it with the one that smells like Sangrash scales or you will be in a mess of trouble."

"I don't know what those are!" Billy said in dismay.

"I don't really know how I'd be able to describe them to you," replied the magician, "They must have such an unusual smell compared to what you must be used to in your world. I don't know what to tell you. The fourth and final ingredient is..." and then his voice grew faint and trailed off into nothingness.

"Nemfootoe?! Are you still there?! Hello?! What about the fourth ingredient?!" Billy called out to him, but there was no answer. The glow from the crystal had faded. "No!" Billy wailed, "Now I'll never know!"

He pulled out the marbles again, but nothing happened. He could do nothing else but put the marbles back into his pocket along with the crystal and continue to the bottle room using the glass piece.

CHAPTER 8

"*How am I to make the potion now?!*" thought Billy, "*I have no idea what all those weird things are or what they smell like. Nemfootoe probably took all the labels off them before the man with no name raided his laboratory. Only he knew which bottles were which. And what about the fourth ingredient?! The energy the marbles gave the crystal ran out before he could tell me what it was! If I go back to the encampment to ask what those things were, what they smell like, the invisibility potion will have worn off and no one will be able to get back into the Ivory Palace again with the creature around. I'll have to guess. I might be able to ask Click to help me too.*"

Billy came to the room with the bottles. He opened the door and put the glass piece back into his pocket. The noise of the door opening must have drawn the creature's attention! Billy heard the sound the beast made as its serpent-like body side-winded down the corridor. It must have been resting in one of the nearby passageways, as Billy could see the beast round the

<A Doorway Of Mirrors><Return To The Ivory Palace> < By Katrina Mandrake-Johnston >< 15 >
corner and approach him and the open door!

Billy was still invisible, and he held his breath and dared not move. The large crocodile head of the creature examined the open doorway in curiosity. Its bird-like talons readjusted their grip along the deadly sharp spear the creature held. Billy was terrified! It was so close! Its eyes were searching for him! Did it know he was there?!

The reptilian beast took its spear and jabbed around in the air near the door! Billy watched the sharp metal tip come towards him! It missed Billy, but only barely.

The creature went past Billy into the bottle room and jabbed around with his spear in there as well. Then, the beast left and continued back down the corridor and out of sight.

Billy breathed a sigh of relief. He didn't dare close the door, not now, and that meant if he asked Click anything, the creature would surely hear and come back. It was already suspicious that someone might be there.

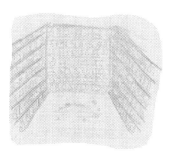

Billy went into the room and looked over the countless shelves for the first ingredient. *"Now what was the bottle supposed to look like?"* Billy asked himself, trying to remember. *"The shape, glass color, liquid color, and the smell,"* Billy said to himself as he searched. *"Okay, I remember now. The first one was… a triangular bottle with green glass, purple liquid inside, and smells like Neefelb berries which are supposed to be sweet and a little bit like freshly cut grass."*

He was glad that he had a good memory. It would be awful if he had forgotten what Nemfootoe had told him, and Billy was glad that he had paid careful attention to his words. He wouldn't have been able to find his way back here if he had just expected Click to show him the way again. He was glad that he had paid close attention to which way they had gone too. It would have wasted precious time speaking to the magician if he had to stop and ask Click which passageway to go down at each junction as well. He might not have found out any of the ingredients if that had happened.

He found a bottle that was triangular-shaped and that had green glass. He reached out with his hand to pick it up off the shelf and noticed that his hand was slowly becoming visible once more. He could see a faint outline of where his hand should be and the color was slowly filling in from the outside edges. If the beast came back to check the room, it would find him now for sure.

Billy opened the bottle, but when he looked inside, he could see that the liquid was bright yellow. It smelt like dandelions and blueberries. He needed one that was purple and that smelt like something similar to grass.

He found another bottle, and Billy opened it to find that it was purple inside, but it had the strong scent of grape jelly and not grass.

Finally, on one of the bottom shelves, he found yet another triangular bottle with green glass. He opened it and was glad to see that it also had purple liquid inside. He held it up to his nose and discovered that this was the one that had the smell of freshly cut grass. Billy had found the first ingredient. He took out the potion bottle Razzmeara had given him.

"Now how much of this was I supposed to put in?" thought Billy, trying very hard to remember correctly. *"Was it halfway full? Was that it? No, I'm sure it wasn't that much. I think it was only to be a fourth of the bottle."*

Billy's mom often had him help her to do the baking. She would get him to measure out the ingredients while she stirred. It helped him with his math at school and it meant he

<A Doorway Of Mirrors><Return To The Ivory Palace> < By Katrina Mandrake-Johnston >< 16 >

would get first pick of the cookies when they were done. It was sure going to help him in this. There were no numbers to guide him on the bottle to help him measure, so he would have to guess.

He held up his finger to where he thought half would be on the rounded bottom of his potion bottle. Then under that, he placed another finger to mark off half of that as well.

Now keeping his bottom finger positioned on the bottle, he took the triangular bottle back off the shelf and carefully poured some of it in to reach to where his finger was, a fourth of the way up. He then corked and put the triangular bottle back on the shelf.

Now Billy had to find the second ingredient. "*For this next one, I'm only supposed to put three drops in. I remember that it was one that had a spiraling neck,*" thought Billy.

He looked around the shelves. He found one that was clear glass and had a round bottom. "*No, wait a minute. That doesn't seem right. It was blue glass, wasn't it?*" Billy asked himself, "*Yeah, it was blue glass and with a square bottom. That's what it was.*"

Billy searched until he found the right bottle. He nervously put three drops of it into his potion. Nemfootoe had warned him to be very careful about how much he put in from this bottle. Billy re-corked it and began his search for the third ingredient.

He listened carefully for the reptilian creature. He was still safe. It didn't seem like it was returning, but Billy would have to hurry. He wasn't invisible anymore and that meant the beast could easily find him. Most likely, the creature would either eat him or take him to the man with no name to become a slave like his sister and grandfather. Billy suspected that the beast wouldn't bother to capture him though. Rashnin had said that this creature would eat anyone it found within the passageways.

"*The third one was short and oval-shaped,*" Billy said to himself, "*Inside is supposed to be a milky white liquid that smells like a weird kind of mushroom. Randosh mushrooms was what I think Nemfootoe said. He also said that, if I confuse it with whatever Sangrash scales are supposed to be, I'll be in a terrible mess.*"

Billy found a short, clear, oval-shaped bottle that had a milky white substance inside. He popped the cork and had a whiff. It smelt horrible; like moldy orange peels and the stinky gym socks that often got left in the change room at school.

"*Maybe this could be it,*" considered Billy. He wanted to ask Click, but he knew the creature would find him if he did. Billy put the cork back into the stinky bottle he had found and searched the shelves to see if he could find another.

He found one quite quickly and opened it up. This one had the same smell that the seaweed baking in the sun at the beach had. "*I better see if there is another bottle to choose from,*" decided Billy.

He scanned the shelves, but there didn't seem to be any other bottles that matched the description. "*So, stinky socks or seaweed,*" thought Billy, "*Which one is it going to be? If I choose the wrong one, it's going to be very bad. The magician warned me about that. Okay, I'm going to have to try to figure this out as best as I can. I wonder if Sangrash scales are from some sort of sea creature. That would have a seaweed-like smell probably. Lots of other things have scales though, and it could be from something in this world that could be so strange that I could never have imagined existed. The Randosh mushrooms might have a moldy orange peel and stinky sock smell, but what if I'm wrong? What if I mix the two bottles up like Nemfootoe warned me not to do? Should I ask Click?*"

Billy heard the sound of the beast sliding across the floor of the corridor. His time had run out! Billy listened… Shhht, shhht, shhht. It was coming closer! Was it coming back to check the room again?!

<A Doorway Of Mirrors><Return To The Ivory Palace> < By Katrina Mandrake-Johnston >< 17 >

Billy quickly went back to get the stinky sock bottle. "*This has to be it… I hope,*" thought Billy, "*I need to fill it until there is only an eighth of the bottle left for the fourth ingredient.*" He poured in the liquid and put the stinky bottle back on the shelf after he had sealed it up again with the cork.

Billy listened… Shhht, shhht, shhht. The creature was still coming this way and it was almost to the room!

"*I don't know what the fourth ingredient is! Should I drink the potion without it? That could be very dangerous. I can't do that!*" Billy thought with worry.

He looked over the bottles frantically, not knowing what to do. "*This is probably exactly what happened to the poor magician! He was making another potion because his had worn off and he was captured before he could use it. He had to smash it so the man with no name couldn't get it.*"

He continued to look over the bottles, his eyes falling on the ones he had already added to his potion. He noticed that most of the dust that had gathered on these bottles had been rubbed off as he had used them. "*Maybe this is a clue! The same thing would have happened when Nemfootoe had made his potion! The last ingredient should have some of the dust smudged off of it. If I find it, I just have to fill my bottle up to the top with it. There might be enough time before the beast comes in here... There! There it is! It must be the one!*" Billy exclaimed when he saw a funny-shaped bottle that had bumpy red glass and almost had the shape of a pineapple.

The dust that had gathered on it had clearly been rubbed off in places. He grabbed it up, popped the cork, and quickly filled his bottle to the top. Billy put the pineapple-shaped bottle back and swished around his own potion slightly before quickly gulping down a big mouthful of it.

"*Did I make it right?*" wondered Billy, "*Did I just poison myself?! I drank some of it without knowing what it would do! I should never have done something like that!*"

Billy waited and listened… Shhht, shhht, shhht. The creature was now in the doorway to the room! Its crocodile head looked from side to side as it searched for him! Billy looked down at himself. It had worked! He was invisible again!

"*What if it comes in here and starts stabbing around with its spear again?! It will get me for sure if it does that!*" Billy thought with fear.

Luckily, the creature turned around and headed back down the passageway once more. Billy needed to get back to Razzmeara to tell her about Nemfootoe and what the marbles had done with the crystal. Most of all, he wanted to tell her that he had made the potion. Billy also wanted to check with her about whether he had chosen the right bottle when he was picking between what he thought Randosh mushrooms and Sangrash scales to smell like. He didn't want to stay invisible forever, if that's what the trouble Nemfootoe was talking about was.

CHAPTER 9

Billy made his way back to the room with the mirror and the stone dragon. There wasn't any sign of the reptilian creature now that he could see. Billy went to the large mirror that kept the doorway there well disguised. The door was still ajar from when he had entered

<A Doorway Of Mirrors><Return To The Ivory Palace> < By Katrina Mandrake-Johnston > < 18 >
the Ivory Palace. He stepped out into the daylight of the warm afternoon.

He had escaped the palace once again. Billy pushed the secret door closed a little way, leaving a small opening for if he ever needed to return that way. There were no handles or any way of reopening the hidden entrance that Billy could see if it did shut all the way.

Still invisible, he traveled across the grassy fields, coming nearer and nearer to the forested area. Billy looked around. There were supposed to be birds to guide him to the hidden entrance to the encampment, but how were they to see that he was returning if he were still invisible?

Would he ever become visible again? He had been walking through the fields for quite awhile and the potion still had not worn off. He only drank a small mouthful; it shouldn't have lasted this long! What if he made the potion wrong?! He felt strange and that feeling had been getting stronger and stronger as he walked. Billy was getting very worried.

He could see the tree line now. The tall grasses in front of him seemed to part for no particular reason at all, as his invisible form waded through them. *"Would Razzmeara's scouts be able to tell it's me?"* Billy wondered, *"Maybe they'll think I'm one of the spies the man with no name has? What if I really am invisible forever?! I'll never get back to Razzmeara then!"*

As Billy reached the forest, he could hear birds chirping within the trees as they darted back and forth among the branches, but none of them seemed to be guiding him in any particular direction. He was still invisible. It was lasting far too long; something must have gone wrong. *"Maybe the potion is lasting longer with a smaller dose just because it was made fresh?"* Billy hoped.

He picked up a fallen tree branch. *"Hopefully, Razzmeara's scouts will see this floating around and realize that it's me. I don't want to call out, as there might be spies about. Both Rashnin and Razzmeara warned me about that. I don't want to give away the secret of where the encampment is."*

Billy remembered the wolf monsters with red eyes he had seen through his mother's magic mirror. They had been chasing after Squeeshna, hunting her down. She had been quick enough to escape them, but there were many people and people-like animals in the encampment that would be too slow to get away. Most of them would be captured if the man with no name sent those terrible creatures down after them.

Billy waved the branch around, hoping to be seen by Razzmeara's scouts. After some time in doing this, a large black crow came to land before him on the forest floor. It turned its head to one side as it examined the branch that was waving about in the air before it.

The bird opened its shiny black beak and cawed loudly. *"Was this crow a friend of Razzmeara's?"* thought Billy nervously.

"Caw!" said the crow.

"Crows, and especially ravens; they are supposed to be extremely intelligent," remembered Billy, *"The crows I've seen back home definitely seem to have their own complex language; calling others to join them in a found meal, warning others of danger, and speaking to each other about who knows what else as they watch us go about our business."*

"Caw, caw!" said the crow, looking at the branch expectantly.

"Ah, hello?" Billy tried as an answer to whatever the crow was saying. He wondered if he had just foolishly given himself away to one of the spies.

"Razzmeara seemed to be part crow though. She had what looked to be a cloak of black feathers draped about her shoulders and down her back, until I found out that they were a part of her," thought Billy.

The crow flew up to land on the nearby lower branch of a small tree. "Caw!" it said

<A Doorway Of Mirrors><Return To The Ivory Palace> < By Katrina Mandrake-Johnston >< 19 >

again, almost with irritation.

"*This must be one of the scouts,*" decided Billy, and holding up his leafy branch, he followed in the direction that the crow had flown.

As soon as he neared where the crow was perched, it cawed at him sharply and took flight to land on yet another branch farther into the trees. So Billy continued to follow the crow until it finally stopped at an incredibly large and ancient tree.

"*This must be the one,*" thought Billy, "*But how can I still be invisible?! Something is definitely wrong, and I feel so dizzy all of a sudden now!*" The crow tapped at the rock near the base of the tree trunk and the secret door opened inwards to reveal the spiraling staircase that led down into the underground encampment.

CHAPTER 10

Billy followed the bird, as it began to hop down the stairs and the hidden entrance shut behind them. As Billy descended, he was relieved to see that he was finally starting to become visible once more. He still felt very dizzy, however, and now he felt incredibly sick to his stomach.

Billy followed the crow to Razzmeara's shop and home within. When they had entered through the open door, the crow gave a loud caw and then flew back out and away from sight.

Razzmeara came forward from behind the counter and hugged him tightly. She had been very worried for her grandson. Her slippery fish-scale arms felt cold against him, but he didn't mind.

"Come Billy, sit down and tell me everything," she said with excitement in her eyes, "Did you find Nemfootoe? Is he all right? Were you able to recreate an invisibility potion? Oh, I am so glad that you have returned safely. I so hated to have to send you out into such danger. Please, tell me everything." Billy came to sit at one of the tables. "Would you like some tea, Billy?"

"Actually, I don't feel so good. I might have mixed the potion wrong," he told her, his stomach feeling as if it were doing somersaults inside of him.

"Oh dear," exclaimed Razzmeara, "I had better get you right into bed then. You should rest. You can tell me all about your adventures a little later."

"Okay," Billy replied weakly, and his grandmother guided him back to the spare room at the back of the shop where he had spent the night before.

Billy laid down upon the bed, without bothering to get under the blankets, and rested his head on the pillow. "Billy, tell me what happened. You said something was wrong with the potion?" Razzmeara asked.

"I found Nemfootoe, but he had his essence trapped within a crystal. I still have it. What happened was the marbles my grandfather left activated the crystal somehow and I was able to talk to the magician. He told me how to make the potion, but I didn't know what some of the things he said were... like weird berries and mushrooms and things. The power ended before he could tell me what the last ingredient was. I found it though, as the bottle had some of the dust smudged off from when Nemfootoe was trying to make his new potion," Billy told

<A Doorway Of Mirrors><Return To The Ivory Palace> < By Katrina Mandrake-Johnston >< 20 >
her.

"But you did turn invisible, did you not?" Razzmeara questioned.

"Yes, but I was worried that I might be stuck that way forever though," mentioned Billy, "What do Randosh mushrooms smell like?"

"Oh, well, John once said that they were similar to this one kind of cheese in his world," Razzmeara replied, "A very strong smell; it is one you definitely notice."

"Like moldy orange peels and stinky socks?" Billy asked, "But not like seaweed, right?"

"Perhaps. It looks like you were able to mix it properly. I doubt you would have become invisible at all if you had not," she explained.

"Why do I feel so strange then?" asked Billy, "Is that normal?"

"I do not think so, but Nemfootoe did not really say anything about the after-effects," she told him. "Oh, your leg!" she gasped, "I'll get some bandages. You have quite a few nasty scrapes around your ankle."

Before he could tell her what had happened with the plant creature, Razzmeara had left the room. Feeling so very weak and tired, Billy had already fallen asleep by the time she returned with the bandages.

CHAPTER 11

When Billy awoke, it was a few hours later. He could smell something cooking that smelt like roast beef and vegetables. Billy's stomach grumbled with hunger. He hadn't had anything to eat since his strange-looking breakfast, and he wondered if dinner would be any different. Razzmeara had wrapped a white cloth-like bandage around his ankle. The scrapes he had gotten from the plant's vine had been itchy a little bit now and then during his journey across the grassy fields and through the forest to get here, but now it was itching like crazy and Billy could see odd-looking bumps underneath the cloth of the bandage.

"Gramma?!" Billy called out, and she came into the room. "Is my leg supposed to itch like this, and what are all these weird bumps? Maybe I'm allergic to what you put on it. Can I take it off?" he asked scratching at the skin around it.

"Oh my," exclaimed Razzmeara, "This should not have happened. I did not apply

anything strange to it. I merely cleaned the area and wrapped a dry strip of cloth around it. You had fallen asleep and I did not want to wake you."

She began unwrapping his ankle, as they both stared in curiosity. The large bumps were revealed to be what looked like brussels sprouts attached to his skin. There were four of them, and Billy's skin had turned green around where they were on his ankle.

Billy looked up at his grandmother in confusion. "What are they?"

"Oh no. They are budlings, Billy," she answered, "But luckily, it looks like the bandage has kept them from escaping."

"Budlings?!" Billy exclaimed, "No wonder why that plant monster seemed to be concerned about me getting eaten by the crocodile creature in the halls."

"He no doubt figured that you would be returning here to me," said Razzmeara, "We have to get these into sealed jars quickly. These would be the reason why you felt ill, Billy."

"Why?! What are they going to do to me?!" Billy asked with worry.

<A Doorway Of Mirrors><Return To The Ivory Palace> < By Katrina Mandrake-Johnston >< 21 >

"Just wait here and I will get the jars. Budlings, as they are called, attach themselves onto someone and use that person's body almost as if they were portable roots. The people would be forced to walk around in order to find better sources of sunlight and water for the budling and would have to stand around in pools of water and out in the sunshine for hours, whether they wanted to or not, and they would not be able to do anything else but stand there under the budling's control," she explained, "Wait here. Do not move, and I will be right back."

Razzmeara quickly left the room and Billy could hear her rummaging around in search for the jars. He stared in disbelief at the round green balls sticking out of his skin. They looked exactly like the brussels sprouts his mom tried to get him to eat on occasion. *"I guess I have one more excuse now for why I hate them,"* thought Billy.

As he stared at his leg, one of the sprouts twitched and two little black eyes opened up to look back at him. Billy didn't know what to do and Razzmeara wasn't back yet with the jars! Another budling opened its eyes, and then another, and another!

"Razzmeara! Hurry! They're waking up!" Billy called out in a panic. With a loud

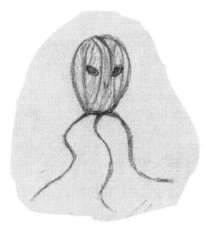

pop, one of the budlings shot out off his leg and across the room.

A second one popped off a second later to land next to Billy on the bed. Three long tendrils were attached at its base and it used these to scramble quickly off the bed and onto the floor like a spider.

Pop! The third was off his leg now and skittering along the floor. "Razzmeara?!" Billy called out.

There was only one more budling left now. Billy watched as it carefully pulled its tendrils out of his leg. The itch was gone now, but his ankle was still a grass-colored green.

This last budling did not scramble to safety on the floor to hide from Razzmeara and her jars when she came. Instead, the budling crawled quickly up Billy's leg. Afraid, he tried to swat it away from him, but it merely jumped over his hand and crawled up to his shoulder. Billy felt the tendrils maneuver down under the collar of his shirt and poke their sharp tips into his shoulder.

"Ow! No! Razzmeara! Help!" cried out Billy. It wiggled its tendrils down beneath his skin until it was firmly attached to him.

CHAPTER 12

Razzmeara sped into the room holding four medium-sized jars with lids. "Billy? Are you all right?" she asked bringing the jars to the bed. "Oh no! Where are the budlings?!" she exclaimed, looking at his bare green ankle.

"They popped off, and one climbed up and worked its way into my shoulder!" Billy told her with tears in his eyes.

"We have to catch them before they get out of the shop!" Razzmeara told him frantically, "The budling on your shoulder won't let you help me, but if you see one, tell me and I will try to get it into a jar."

"What if one attaches to you, Gramma? Then they'll get out for sure!" said Billy.

<A Doorway Of Mirrors><Return To The Ivory Palace> < By Katrina Mandrake-Johnston >< 22 >

"They cannot harm me, Billy. Do not worry about that. We must catch them all before they get out or they will indeed spread like that. Anyone trying to catch one will most likely have it attach to them. Worst of all, for them to create more of themselves, they will bring people to the large plant you encountered for him to eat. They call him their father. They speak through telepathy; their words are heard within your mind even though they make no sound themselves. Once their father consumes someone, he is able to make more of his budlings. That means that the budling returning to the father will need to capture someone else that doesn't already have one in order for that person to bring the new budlings back with him just as you have done."

"Yes, he ate the servant that was taking Nemfootoe's crystal to the man with no name. That's how I was able to get the magician's shard. Oh, I see one! It just ran under the table there! Do you see it?! Wow, they sure move fast!"

They heard a rattling sound from in the other room. "Sounds like the other two are already hiding in among the shelves of the shop," said Razzmeara, "This is not going to be an easy task, and if they get out of this building, we are all going to be in big trouble."

"What if the one on my shoulder makes me kidnap someone to take back to the Ivory Palace?! I don't want to do something like that! The crocodile monster there will eat both of us anyway, and if we get past it, the plant monster will eat me to put his budlings into whomever I bring with me! Don't let that happen! Please!"

"First I have to find and catch them," she told him, "We stopped his budlings once, and we can do it again."

"How?" he asked her, as she started to creep toward the table where the budling was hiding.

"We have a lot of them living harmlessly in jars now. We make sure they have plenty of water and light, and they are where they cannot do any more damage. I did not want to have them destroyed, although many of the people that had suffered under them wanted them to be. To do that would have been wrong."

Razzmeara leapt towards the budling with her jar and its lid but missed. The budling skittered into the shop area, and Billy heard the rattle of bottles and the sound of one falling to the floor to break. She grabbed up the jars from Billy's bed and hurried into the other room.

CHAPTER 13

Shortly after Razzmeara had left, Billy heard a squeaky little voice say, "Please, do not let us be put into jars." It was the budling on his shoulder that had spoken to him.

"You're going to hurt others! You're going to make me take people to the big plant trapped in the palace! You're going to make me stand around in a pool of water all day in the sun, living like a plant instead of a person!" he said angrily to the budling.

"No, please. I don't want that to happen either," the budling told him, "That is what father wants to do, not me or my three brothers here. We sat with father for many days and nights. I don't want to force someone to do something they don't want to do. Father wouldn't listen, no matter what I said though. I told him that if we try to find people that are willing to take care of us instead of forcing them to, that we could live peacefully and not fight against the queen and her subjects. We want to bond with someone so we can see the world. None of us want to be put into a jar instead. Father was the one that wanted to take over the world, not us. Please Billy, give us a chance to show that we don't want to hurt anyone. We do not need to make new budlings; there are enough of us already. We can transfer easily to someone new, if someone gets too old to care for us or simply doesn't want to anymore. Father is locked up

<A Doorway Of Mirrors><Return To The Ivory Palace> < By Katrina Mandrake-Johnston >< 23 >
in the Ivory Palace and he can stay there for all the evil he's tried to do. If Razzmeara ever returns to be queen in the Ivory Palace, she can keep us budlings away from him and see that we don't want to cause any trouble. Please Billy, give us a chance, please?"

"This sounds like a trick. Let me talk to Razzmeara. Let me get up off this bed. What is to stop the budlings from taking over the people once they are bonded with them? It's a trick, isn't it?" said Billy.

"It is up to you. Trust only me then. I cannot speak for all of the budlings. Some of them might feel the same way that father does. Please, let me travel with you. You can always send me into a jar with the others later. Please, give me a chance?" the budling pleaded.

Billy was able to get up off the bed; the budling had let him. He ran into the other room where Razzmeara was capturing the last budling. "Wow, you caught them all already?" Billy exclaimed.

"Billy, you got the one off your shoulder then?" she asked him.

"No, he's still there," Billy told her, "He says that he wants to have peace. Go ahead and tell her what you told me."

The budling explained to Razzmeara what he had said to Billy. "What do you think?" asked Billy.

"Well, if he is telling the truth, I would certainly agree to having peace with the budlings. However, there is too much risk involved. Billy, if you want to give this single budling a chance to prove himself, then so be it. I cannot release the others, however, until I know for certain that they mean no harm," explained the queen.

There came a knock at the front door of the shop. Razzmeara opened it to see Rashnin along with an odd-looking creature that looked like a white bug with two long spindly

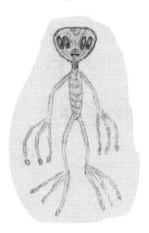

legs and arms. This bug-like being had a round head with four big eyes, two on either side of its face. It had a small thin mouth and a short little body. It nervously twitched its long fingers and toes as it stood there beside Rashnin. "May we come in? There seems to be an urgent matter we should discuss in private," the hedgehog explained. The two of them entered the shop and Razzmeara shut the door behind them.

"Rashnin, what is going on?" the queen asked him.

Rashnin rustled his hedgehog-like prickly spines and his nose began to twitch on the end of his long snout. "This creature says he was one of the ones that lived here long ago. The beetle riders that mysteriously disappeared," he told them.

CHAPTER 14

"Please, come sit down. May I offer you something to drink?" she asked the strange creature. It shook its large wobbly head, but decided to sit upon a chair at a nearby table.

"My name is Beeshum," the creature told them, "My people are being held captive in the tunnels and are being made to dig and collect crystals for the man with no name."

"How did you escape?" asked Razzmeara.

<A Doorway Of Mirrors><Return To The Ivory Palace> < By Katrina Mandrake-Johnston >< 24 >

"I suppose I was lucky, I guess," replied Beeshum nervously.

"So we know now where he gets the crystals he uses to create his slaves," commented Rashnin, "Now if there is only some way to stop him from getting them."

"Yes," said Razzmeara, "If he is unable to get new crystals, he will be unable to make new slaves. Tell us more about what goes on within the tunnels."

"We are to place the crystals we collect upon a shiny metal platform. They disappear into it and are sent to where the man with no name wants them to go," Beeshum told them.

"I was transported like that from the field where I was trying to get the herbs with Squeeshna. I sank right into the metal and ended up in a prison cell in the Ivory Palace," said Billy.

"Who or what is it that is holding your people captive?" asked Rashnin, "Surely, it is not the man with no name himself."

Beeshum began to cry big yellowy tears from all four of his big blue eyes. "He used to be our friend! He would look after all of us in a way. Now, he is something else; something twisted and evil! The man with no name did something to him; changed him somehow."

"What, did he turn him into a slave or something?" asked Billy.

Razzmeara brought a handkerchief over to Beeshum. He accepted it and dried his tears. "How about that cup of tea I mentioned earlier?" she asked him with a smile.

He nodded his wobbly head and his thin little mouth turned up in a polite smile. As she prepared the tea behind the counter, Billy stared at the three budlings within the jars.

"I would not mention the trouble we have just had with those," she whispered to Billy, "They are safe where they are now and we do not need to frighten the people here in the encampment about them, at least not yet."

Billy nodded. Everyone had enough to worry about with all that the man with no name had caused. He knew that Razzmeara would warn everyone if these new budlings became a threat. He wondered what was to happen to him because of the one on his shoulder. Billy's budling seemed to be cooperating so far.

Razzmeara placed a steaming cup of tea in front of everyone. It smelt delicious; like peaches and raspberries, but it was far too hot to drink yet.

"Thank-you," said Beeshum and he went on to say, "He is a being that is in most part fungus. What I mean is that he looks like a large mushroom for most of the time, but on occasion, he can change his form into a more humanoid appearance. Since the man with no name did whatever he did to him, he has not changed and has not spoken to us. He attacks us with his spores if we do not dig for crystals. It's awful, and his spores burn us like fire when he releases them. Our friend is not a slave like the others; just different."

"I heard that the land, some of the animals and vegetation, were mutated and changed by the man with no name, turning peaceful beings into monsters," Billy mentioned, "Maybe that's what happened."

"There are these strange mushrooms that grew at all the entrances to the network of inner tunnels. They keep us from escaping. He probably has something to do with them as well," said Beeshum, as he nervously took a sip of the tea, "Simpar; that's our friend I was telling you about. He is guarding an amulet too, although I don't know what it could be for. It glows with a magical energy."

"Does it have a red stone?" asked Razzmeara, taking a sip from her cup. Beeshum nodded his wobbly head again and took a big noisy slurp of tea. "I know what that amulet is then," said the queen.

"So do I," added in Rashnin.

<A Doorway Of Mirrors><Return To The Ivory Palace> < By Katrina Mandrake-Johnston >< 25 >

"What? What is it?" asked Billy, finishing his tea in one gulp.

"Remember the dragon, Billy?" said Rashnin, "That's the amulet the man with no name used to turn him to stone. If we can get that, we can restore him to normal and take back the Ivory Palace."

"I could show you the way, Billy," offered Beeshum, "We might be able to get the amulet with your help."

"I don't know if that's a good idea, Billy," said Rashnin.

Beeshum noticed the jars on the counter and said, "I've seen those before! We uncovered a whole room full of them."

"Your people must have tunneled into the lower chambers in the Ivory Palace," Razzmeara told him, "It seems your tunnels are quite extensive."

"What about the beetles?" inquired Rashnin, "What of them?"

"We haven't seen them in a long time. I suspect they are also being held captive in another part of the underground," he answered.

"I could do it. I could try to help," offered Billy, "I can escape back through the Ivory Palace with the invisibility potion, if I can't get past the mushroom barriers."

"So tell me again," said Razzmeara rather sternly, "How did you get past to escape?"

"I…" Beeshum started to say, and tears ran down his white cheeks, "The man with no name has my family."

"What was the deal you made with him?" she asked firmly.

Beeshum answered, "I was to bring Billy; he showed me what he looked like and everything. I was to bring him into the tunnels and past the mushrooms, so he would become trapped there along with my people. I'm sorry. He said that if I did that, he would free my family from being slaves, but that they would merely be sent back to dig for crystals with the rest of us. We would at least be together again that way. But now there could be a way for both of us. I could get my family back, and then, Billy could escape. The man with no name won't know that he is able to escape back through the palace once he has entered the tunnel network."

Rashnin told them, "It would mean that he would think Billy is imprisoned and no longer a threat to his plans. He might begin to let his guard down a little after that. It might help. But I doubt he would release Beeshum's family once he has what he wants."

"I know, but I have to try," Beeshum explained, "and maybe there's a chance we can get the amulet too."

"I could take the jars to the room with the others," said Billy.

"No, not you," said Razzmeara, "It would be safer if Beeshum carried them. That way the one you have will be unable to release them."

"Wait a minute," Rashnin said, "Razzmeara, those aren't what I think they are, are they?"

"I am afraid so, but it will be all right," she assured him, "We should make arrangements for your departure. Billy, are you sure you want to do this?"

Billy nodded, and Beeshum collected up the jars into an empty sack on the counter. Billy hugged Razzmeara good-bye, and Rashnin escorted him and Beeshum through the encampment on their way to the underground tunnels.

CHAPTER 15

"This is it," Beeshum told them, "Rashnin, I'm sorry, but Billy and I will have to carry on without you from here."

<A Doorway Of Mirrors><Return To The Ivory Palace> < By Katrina Mandrake-Johnston >< 26 >

Before them, on either side of the path, were mushrooms of all manner of shape, color, and size.

"So what do these mushrooms do exactly? They look harmless enough," said Billy.

"That is in where the trap lies," explained Beeshum, "They will let you pass by them going into the inner tunnels, but if anyone tries to come back out, they sense the movement somehow and release a tremendous haze that actually pushes you backwards with an incredible force. It must be some sort of magic that causes them to be able to do that. All I know is that no one has been able to make it past them. I was allowed to, only because I had agreed to help the man with no name by bringing you here."

"What did the room with the budlings look like?" asked Rashnin suspiciously.

"I'm telling you the truth! Do you think I would truly want to help that monster, the man with no name?! It is not a trick; there really is a tunnel that leads into the palace. There are terrible creatures lurking about in the palace, however, and I will not take you in past the mushrooms unless you are sure that you can make it safely out that way."

"We've both seen that reptilian monster in the halls there," commented Billy.

"Oh, there are many more than simply that one creature," Beeshum warned, "If you are to do this, you must understand that there will be many unexpected dangers and terrible beasts in there now that the man with no name has taken over. The lower levels are probably the worst. Many of us tried to escape through the palace when we became trapped in the tunnels. Only a few ever made it back out alive and none of us managed to make it out to the surface levels."

"I have an invisibility potion, and I will try my best," Billy said bravely.

"Okay, follow me then. Know that your potion won't work against Simpar, he'll be able to sense your movements without needing to see you. We will have to find some other way for getting the amulet away from him," explained Beeshum, and he stepped in-between the mushroom clusters on either side of the path. The mushrooms expanded their tops, and a thick grey mist arose from them. Beeshum was then sent sprawling into the other room as the force of the magical cloud slammed into him.

"Are you all right?" Billy called out.

"Yes, I'm fine," he replied.

"What about my brothers?" the budling asked in a squeaky whisper to Billy.

"In the sack, the plants inside the jars, are they okay?" Billy asked for him.

"Yes, I managed to keep them safe when I fell," Beeshum called back.

"Good-bye, Rashnin," said Billy.

He nuzzled his long hedgehog snout affectionately into Billy's hand. "I shall forever

<A Doorway Of Mirrors><Return To The Ivory Palace> < By Katrina Mandrake-Johnston >< 27 >

be grateful for you rescuing me from the prison cell in the palace," said Rashnin, "I wish you the best of luck, and please take care, Billy."

Billy held his breath and stepped forward onto the path between the mushrooms. The haze rose up, and Billy was pushed forward just as Beeshum had been.

Beeshum was waiting for him and he helped Billy to his feet after he had landed in the room beyond the mushrooms. There were many different tunnels branching off from this small chamber. Beeshum directed him along the many different passageways and junctions, leading him farther and farther into the network of tunnels.

CHAPTER 16

Soon, Beeshum had led him down so many twists and turns, and through so many tunnels that all seemed alike, that Billy became hopelessly lost. He was blindly following Beeshum and having to completely rely on him.

"How can you tell where you're going?" asked Billy, "All these tunnels look the same to me."

"Oh no, the Deershirnt root patterns are different in each passageway. With time, you learn to recognize what tunnel leads where," he explained.

"What roots?" Billy asked in confusion, looking around.

"Look up," Beeshum told him, "They are what provide light to these underground walkways."

As Billy examined overhead, he said with surprise, "I thought that the light from above was just filtering down through ventilation holes or something. That's what Razzmeara told me earlier. I don't believe it! There are actually squiggly glowing roots poking through along the roof here and there."

Beeshum explained, "The plants absorb sunlight during the day and moonlight at night. The entire plant radiates a glow because of it. The roots of a Deershirnt plant are extremely long, as you can see, and it is the roots that are the brightest. We can tell night and day by how brightly the roots are glowing. Most important to us is that they are not only our source of light, but also our source of fresh air down here. The roots give off a large amount of oxygen. I've even heard of people using them in underwater vessels to provide them with light and air. Anyway, we are fortunate that they grow in such abundance here, as we are far too deep to be able to rely on anything else. I don't think you realize just how far we have come already. Razzmeara was correct in what she said, but that was far above in the encampment near the surface."

Billy was led down a few more passageways, and then Beeshum announced in a whisper, "We're just about there now. This tunnel will eventually open up into the large chamber that is pretty much the center of the network, and most of the tunnels branch out from there. This is where we'll find Simpar."

Soon they came to stand on a narrow ledge, and reminding Billy of the grooves on a screw, he saw that the ledge wound all around the bowl-like chamber and continued its way to the other tunnel entrances that were higher up here. Billy and Beeshum had come out near the bottom of the chamber floor.

Before them in the center of the room was an enormous mushroom, much like the smaller ones that they had seen earlier. It had a thick stalk with a large dome-like top, the underside of which was lined with grey-colored slats. Hanging down from the outer rim of the mushroom, however, were countless little tube-like growths. Red and purple splotches covered the yellowy-white flesh of the mushroom top.

<A Doorway Of Mirrors><Return To The Ivory Palace> < By Katrina Mandrake-Johnston >< 28 >

As Billy stared in amazement, Beeshum explained, "When Simpar is in this fungus-like state, he can release spores through those tubes there on the outer brim. Underneath the mushroom top is where he collects his air by flexing those grey membranes there. The stalk is very tough and very sturdy, so even if we were to attack our dear friend in his entranced state caused by the man with no name, it would do no good. In this fungus form he does not need to use his eyes; Simpar will be able to sense us. Keep in mind that although he looks like a mushroom, that he is not entirely so. He will behave very differently."

"I understand," said Billy.

"There has to be a way to eventually free him. If we can get through all this without hurting him…" Beeshum said sadly.

"I know. Even though he is the one keeping your people here and making you work to collect the crystals, it is definitely not Simpar who is the villain here," stated Billy.

"The amulet is lodged at the top of the dome-like top of the mushroom," Beeshum told him, "A few of us tried to jump down from one of the upper ledges, trying to land on Simpar and take the amulet away from him, but it didn't work. He sent up a cloud much like the mushrooms we encountered earlier. As soon as someone jumps, they are pushed away."

"What about a ladder? Someone could climb up and then be able to hang on and crawl their way to the amulet," suggested Billy.

"That could work, as his blast of air is not as strong as the smaller ones. Someone might be able to hold on once on top. However, if anyone gets close, Simpar releases those spores that irritate your skin as if they were made of fire. The pain is too much to take. Besides, no one could endure a full attack from the spores. So far he has just been releasing mild warnings; a full blast of them could kill," Beeshum warned him gravely.

"So what should we do then?" asked Billy.

"I don't know," answered Beeshum, "I suppose we take these plants to the room with the others; and then I take you to Simpar to see if the man with no name is truly going to release and return my family to me."

"I don't really like that idea," said Billy nervously.

"Neither do I!" added in the budling on his shoulder.

"Who said that?!" Beeshum asked in astonishment. Billy pulled back the collar of his shirt to expose the little budling attached there. "Is that one of those plants, like the ones in the jars? They're intelligent?! Did it just talk to us?" he asked in amazement.

"Yes, but apparently they caused a lot of trouble in the past. This one wants to change that and come to peaceful terms instead," Billy explained, "I guess they don't talk much when they're stuck in the jars."

"I'll show you to the room then," Beeshum told him, "That way, if you need to find it

<A Doorway Of Mirrors><Return To The Ivory Palace> < By Katrina Mandrake-Johnston >< 29 >
on your own to escape that way, you can."

"Sounds good," agreed Billy, and they made their way up going around and around the chamber, walking up the ledge and passing by numerous tunnel entrances until they were at the very top.

"This is it," Beeshum told Billy, "Just follow it all the way in and you'll get there."

It was very bright near the top here, as the Deershirnt roots were densely clustered and filling the entire room with their light. Billy looked over the side of the narrow ledge and saw how very high up he was. He could see the mushroom below and the glint of the amulet.

"Do you think it's the amulet that is turning your friend bad? Maybe if we remove it, he'll be fine," suggested Billy.

"Unfortunately no. He was given the amulet long after he was changed into this monster by the man with no name," answered Beeshum sadly, "We should be on our way then and at least get the sack with the jars to safety before confronting Simpar."

Billy nodded and followed him into the tunnel.

CHAPTER 17

Soon they came to a room that had smooth white walls, and Billy knew that they had reached the Ivory Palace. In the ceiling were tiny holes, and Beeshum explained that several times a day, water would be released down onto the floor where all the jars were positioned. It would then seep in through the holes in the lids to water the plants. The walls seemed to glow, providing the room with the light the plants needed. Billy hadn't really thought about it, but when he had been in the upper hallways of the Ivory Palace, there hadn't been any light fixtures of any kind. It was probably the same there as well. In one corner of the room, a narrow wooden ladder was propped up against the wall.

"So there's a ladder there," mentioned Beeshum, "But I don't think it would be a good idea to try to climb up onto Simpar with it. If he releases a cloud of spores to attack you, it could be fatal."

Beeshum reached his long, thin white fingers into the sack and began to set the jars from it out onto the floor with the other budlings. Billy awkwardly picked up the ladder and brought it out of the room and back into the tunnel.

"Hey, wait for me," Beeshum called after him, as he hurried after Billy.

"I have to try," said Billy bravely, "I can at least bring it down to the bottom of the chamber and then hope that we can come up with a better plan in the meantime." Beeshum grabbed the other end of the ladder and helped Billy to carry it down the winding ledge to the chamber floor below where Simpar was.

They laid the ladder upon the ground, and then both stood before the giant mushroom. "I have Billy!" Beeshum called out loudly to Simpar, "He is trapped within the tunnels with no way out. I have done as the man with no name has asked. I await the return of my family." With all four of his large blue eyes, Beeshum looked to Billy and whispered, "Now we wait and see what happens. See the metal platform there, a little ways off near the stalk of the mushroom?"

Billy nodded, and they both waited. The platform began to shimmer and something started to rise up out of the liquidly metal. It was the shape of a person, and as the metal flowed back down into the platform off this person, Billy gasped in astonishment. He stared in disbelief as the person stepped off the platform and onto the dirt floor of the chamber.

"Jenny?! Is it really you?!" Billy exclaimed.

"I knew it!" remarked Beeshum angrily, "He was never going to release my family

<A Doorway Of Mirrors><Return To The Ivory Palace> < By Katrina Mandrake-Johnston >< 30 >
back to me!" Billy rushed forward towards Jenny. He had found her! "Billy! No!" Beeshum called out with fear, "It's her, but it's a trap! She's a slave!"

Jenny stepped backwards onto the platform and sank quickly away. Beeshum was right; it was a trap. Billy was now closer to the mushroom and right below where he could receive a full blast from Simpar's spores. The man with no name had lured him in to where he simply had no chance of outrunning the explosion of spores in time.

Simpar shuddered and a thick red cloud erupted from each of the tubes along the mushroom's edge. Billy fell to the ground in that deadly eruption. Beeshum cried out in horrible pain as the spores attacked his skin, and he ran quickly away to cower at the entrance to one of the bottom tunnels.

"Billy! No! It's all my fault! I should have never brought him here!" Beeshum wailed.

Feeling dizzy and disorientated, Billy got back up, and as he stood there, he watched as the red mist billowed about him. He could see nothing but the thick red cloud surrounding him. Amazingly, he was not killed by the spores. They did not even sting his skin in the

slightest. "How is this possible?" said Billy in wonderment.

"Perhaps it is me?" commented the budling on his shoulder.

"What? Really?" asked Billy with surprise.

"We must be creating an air space as a natural defense mechanism," said the budling, "I guess it's similar to how the smaller mushrooms were able to hit us with that blast of mist. I didn't know that we could do that; produce an air pocket like this. You see, what I haven't told you is that your body has been quickly changing since I first attached myself to you," the budling explained, "Don't worry, it is nothing that will hurt you. You are becoming part of me, as I am becoming part of you. For example, you will start to sprout fuzzy little roots from the bottom of your feet."

"What?!" exclaimed Billy in horror.

"Well yes, remember Razzmeara said that the people that had budlings would stand around in water all day?" reminded the budling, "The roots on the bottom of their feet allow for the water to be absorbed. Don't worry Billy, if I need to drink, I'll let you know and trust that you will take care of me."

"You promise that nothing bad will come of this? The roots on my feet are the only thing that will happen?" asked Billy nervously.

"Yes, you won't even know they are there. All they might do is tickle a little bit now and then," the budling assured him.

Just then, as he stood within the cloud of spores, a wonderful idea came to Billy, "Hey, if you can keep the spores from hurting me, maybe I can get the amulet!"

"I have a better idea, Billy," said the budling.

CHAPTER 18

"What?" he asked the budling.

"Well, if I can keep the spores from hurting you, the same can happen for Beeshum and his people," the budling explained, "The threat of the spores is the only reason why they have been forced to collect crystals for the man with no name, right? It won't matter if they stop, because the budlings will keep them safe."

<A Doorway Of Mirrors><Return To The Ivory Palace> < By Katrina Mandrake-Johnston >< 31 >

"And if the man with no name can't get new crystals, he can't make any new slaves," exclaimed Billy with excitement, "That's a great idea! Oh, but wait. What if the other budlings start to take over as they had done before?"

"If my brothers or I talk to them, I'm sure they'll listen," said the budling with confidence, "I'm sure my three brothers are discussing the situation and our plan for peace with them all even as we speak."

"Well, I guess it's worth a try, if we can stop the man with no name from enslaving anyone else and keep Beeshum's people from harm until we find a way to turn Simpar back to normal," said Billy, "We should grab the ladder and get the amulet. The spore cloud is clearing up now; we'll be able to see unless Simpar releases more. I wonder if Beeshum is all right?"

As Billy stepped away from Simpar, Beeshum called out with delight and surprise, "Billy! You're okay! How did you survive?!"

Billy said to him, "I'll tell you in a minute. I'm going to get the amulet before he can shoot out any more spores."

Billy picked up the ladder from the ground and Beeshum ran over to him. Large red splotches could be seen on Beeshum's white skin where the spores had hurt him. "Are you all right?" Billy asked him with concern.

"I'll be okay. I can hold the ladder while you climb up. Simpar won't be able to send out more for a little while. This is your chance!"

With Beeshum holding the bottom of the ladder steady, Billy climbed up to the top where he could get onto the rubbery flesh of the mushroom. "Are you all right?" Beeshum called up to him.

"Yeah, but it's a little slippery up here," he called back, scrambling to keep his balance on the mushroom's flesh.

"You better lie flat and crawl, or else he can knock you over with a blast of force like the smaller ones could," Beeshum warned.

Billy started to crawl along, and after a few feet, a strong gust of air that smelt like stinky socks blew up out of a million tiny pores on the mushroom's top. He grabbed hold as best as he could, lying flat against it until the rush of air had passed.

Billy continued along the mushroom until he could see the amulet. Simpar released another gust of air and Billy was almost pushed off. Once it had passed, Billy reached forward and grabbed hold of the amulet. It was stuck deeply into the flesh of the mushroom, but Billy was able to yank it free. He slid back down to the ladder and quickly climbed to the bottom where Beeshum awaited him.

"I have it!" Billy grinned, holding it up by its silver chain. The red gem set into the small gold triangle sparkled in the strange light from the Deershirnt roots above. "Come on, let's get up to the Ivory Palace room. The budling is what saved me from the spores, maybe they can do the same for you and your people. That way the man with no name can't get any more crystals; and that means, no more new slaves."

<A Doorway Of Mirrors><Return To The Ivory Palace> < By Katrina Mandrake-Johnston >< 32 >

"Okay, but he will become suspicious after awhile and will come to suspect that you were not killed after all," Beeshum warned.

When they had returned to the room with the budling jars, Beeshum took the lid off one of the jars he had brought there earlier from the sack and that contained one of the budling's brothers.

"I hope you're right about this, Billy," said Beeshum, and he put the budling onto his thin white shoulder. "Ow!" he exclaimed as it poked its tendrils into his skin. "Okay, if it works for me as well, I'll tell the others to do the same. We still won't be able to leave the tunnels because of the mushroom barriers, but at least the spores won't be able to hurt us anymore. If you can make it to the room with the stone dragon using your invisibility potion, I'm sure you'll be able to turn him back to normal with that amulet. That dragon will chase any monsters lurking about out of the Ivory Palace for good. Razzmeara and her people could reclaim the palace for their own once more, if that happens. You are already a hero to us, Billy. Thank-you."

Billy hoped that the budling wasn't tricking them into releasing the other budlings, but they had to take that chance. The man with no name had to be stopped from getting new crystals and this was the only way. Billy hoped he didn't have a very large supply of crystals stored up already. The budlings would be trapped in the tunnels just as Beeshum and his people were, but they did have access to the Ivory Palace and that was where their father was being held captive in the room near Nemfootoe's entranced body. If Billy could free the dragon, however, and return Razzmeara and her people to the Ivory Palace, they could make sure that no one under the control of a budling could go up to that room with the large father plant.

Billy couldn't see a door anywhere, but then he remembered the glass piece. When he held it up to his eye, he could see the door that Beeshum and his people must have found on their own. Billy waved good-bye to Beeshum and went through the door and farther into the Ivory Palace.

CHAPTER 19

Billy was in a narrow passageway, and through his glass piece, he could see that many other passageways branched off to the left and right farther along the corridor. He rummaged around in his pocket until he found Click. Billy took him out and Click rolled his little metallic eyes around to see where they were this time.

"Hi Click," said Billy, "I'm going to need your help again little friend. We're back in the Ivory Palace and we need to get back to the room with the stone dragon. It's going to be a few floors up, I think. Do you think you can help me find it?"

"Buzz click click," answered Click, meaning yes.

"Can you just tell me if I'm going the right way, or do I have to ask you every time?" asked Billy, hoping he could, as to ask Click about every possible direction for each junction was very time-consuming.

<A Doorway Of Mirrors><Return To The Ivory Palace> < By Katrina Mandrake-Johnston >< 33 >

"Buzz click click," he said.

"Oh wait," said Billy, realizing that he had asked two different questions instead of one, "So you can just tell me, without me having to ask?"

"Buzz click click," replied Click, moving his eyes about again.

Billy started to walk down the corridor, holding the glass piece up before his eye. He wondered if he should take drink of the potion. *"I don't want to be invisible for too long. What if I'm still invisible when I free the dragon? He might roast me with fire, thinking I'm working for the man with no name or even by accident if he can't see me and I get in the way. He is supposed to be a good dragon, isn't he? What if he is like a guard dog without his master? What if he can't understand what I have to say?"*

Billy passed by many different passageways and a few doors, but kept continuing on straight along the corridor. Click, resting on Billy's outstretched palm, suddenly said, "Buzz buzz."

Billy stopped and took a step toward the passageway on the left. "Buzz buzz," said Click.

Billy turned around and headed down the passageway on the right. "Buzz click click," he told him.

"Thanks Click!" Billy said to him, "That's much easier and faster."

Soon Billy and Click came to where the passageway they were on turned to the left

and led into a large circular room. A narrow staircase leading up to another floor could be seen at the back of the room. However, asleep on the floor in the middle of the room was a terrifying creature. It looked like one of the wolf-like monsters Billy had seen through his mother's magic mirror that had been chasing after Squeeshna. Its large head rested on its paw, where Billy could see huge dagger-like claws. Its long shaggy fur was thick and black. Drool had dribbled down from its huge jaws full of large jagged teeth. In fear, Billy watched the creature breathe; its chest moving up and down as it slept and with its wide shiny nose wiggling as the air escaped its lungs in a low whistle.

Billy slowly backed away to hide around the corner back within the corridor. "I better take some of the potion now," Billy whispered to Click, "It's too dangerous for us to try to sneak past. But, this time instead of taking a big gulp, I'll just take a few drops. Hopefully that way, it will wear off by the time we reach the dragon. I'll put you back in my pocket so you'll be safe, Click, okay?"

After Billy had placed Click back in his pocket, he took out his invisibility potion. He put three drops of it onto his tongue and waited.

After a few moments, the magic began to work and he started to disappear.

Billy crept back into the room with the wolf beast. He slowly began to edge his way along the wall around the creature.

Suddenly, the monster awoke; its fiery red eyes seeming to burn with malice. It lifted up its large head and snapped its jaws together a few times making a hollow clacking sound with

<A Doorway Of Mirrors><Return To The Ivory Palace> < By Katrina Mandrake-Johnston >< 34 >
its teeth. It started to sniff at the air. Billy hugged the wall, his back tightly against it, too frightened to move. It continued to sniff about in the air, its red eyes searching.

Finally, it laid its head back down to rest once again on its paw. It closed its eyes, and after awhile, the air began to whistle through its black nose with each deep heaving breath once more. The creature had fallen back to sleep.

Billy slowly and quietly continued to edge his way around the room, and finally he reached the staircase. He hurried up the stairs, away from the creature, and up to the floor above.

CHAPTER   20

"How close are we to the dragon room, Click? Are we on the right floor now?" Billy asked, taking him out.

"Buzz click click," he told him.

"Great, then we're almost there!" said Billy, "But, that also means that this is the floor where the reptilian creature lurks within the halls. It's a good thing we're invisible now. We should hurry before it wears off. A few drops probably aren't going to last very long. You can guide me like you did before, to go fast?"

"Buzz click click," answered Click, meaning yes.

They maneuvered down the passageways, getting closer and closer to the room with the stone dragon. Billy had to be very careful not to accidentally drop Click. If that ever happened, Click would not only get hurt, but Billy would never be able to find him as he too was invisible right now. There didn't seem to be any sign of the reptilian creature, but Billy didn't let his guard down, as the beast had seemed to come out of nowhere the time before when Billy thought he was safe back at the bottle room.

Soon they had reached the room, and Billy stood before the massive stone dragon. The door behind the large mirror was just as he had left it. The hidden entrance looked as if it were still a secret. Billy put the glass piece back in his pocket, as he didn't need it anymore here in this room. He also put Click back in as well, so he would be kept safe. Billy felt around until he found the amulet. He brought it out and stepped up to the dragon. It towered above him, almost to the ceiling.

"*What do I do with it?*" Billy asked himself. As Billy pondered what he should do next, he slowly started to become visible once more. He looked nervously around for the creature, but he was safe for now.

"*Maybe if I just touch him with it,*" thought Billy, "*I guess it's worth a try.*" He touched the red gem of the amulet to the cold grey stone of the dragon's leg. "*I don't want to do something wrong with it. I could easily get turned to stone as well,*" thought Billy nervously.

He put the amulet back into his pocket. "*Well, I guess that didn't work. I should probably head back to the encampment to ask Razzmeara what to do. Oh, but I don't know the way!*" Billy thought with frustration, "*The crow showed me the time before. They don't know I'll be returning this way or when I would be if they did know. Maybe Click can show me the way.*"

The stone began to crack with an awful snapping sound. "Oh no, what did I do?!" exclaimed Billy.

<A Doorway Of Mirrors><Return To The Ivory Palace> < By Katrina Mandrake-Johnston >< 35 >

The stone continued to crack with great lines breaking up and out across the entire form of the dragon. Billy jumped back as pieces began to fall away to land on the white floor of the chamber.

"The reptilian creature will surely hear this!" thought Billy, *"It's a good thing the secret doorway is so near."*

As more of the stone fell away, Billy realized that there were dark green scales beneath. The entire stone dragon wasn't breaking apart; it was only a thin layer of rock that encased the dragon within. The stone skin was coming off and the dragon was being freed. What Billy had done with the amulet had worked!

Soon the dragon was completely free, with a pile of rubble around him. He stretched out his massive bat-like wings as best as he could in the cramped room, as it was for such a large beast.

Billy was suddenly very afraid. "Razzmeara sent me! Please don't eat me!" Billy called out.

The dragon bent down its large head. It was much like that of a crocodile, just like the reptilian beast, only the dragon's head was much broader and it had large pointed ears like a cat. To Billy's relief, the dragon spoke, saying, "I'm not going to eat you." The dragon's deep voice rumbled like thunder and sent shivers down Billy's back.

Shhht, shhht, shhht. Billy heard the reptilian creature making its way to the room. "There's this monster in the halls! It's coming! What should I do?!"

"Get behind me. I'll deal with him," bellowed the dragon.

CHAPTER 21

Billy scrambled over the pile of rocks to hide in the corner of the room. The

crocodile beast stood at the entrance to the room holding its spear in its bird-like talons. The dragon inhaled and let loose a massive blast of fire at the crocodile creature. However, the flames were blue, and they did not seem to be burning the beast. The creature seemed to be changing within the dragon's flames.

Once the dragon's breath had subsided, what stood in the doorway was a toad that was almost as large as Billy. The spear was lying harmlessly on the ground beside the toad. It let out a low croak, then said "Thank-you," and hopped away down the corridor.

"You're able to reverse what the man with no name has done to some of the creatures, the ones that have been changed and not made into slaves?" questioned Billy.

"That is correct," answered the dragon in his deep rumbling voice.

"Then it will be safe for Razzmeara and her people to return to the Ivory Palace, right?" asked Billy with hope.

"Yes," replied the dragon.

"There are others," Billy told him, "There is a big wolf beast on the lower level by the stairs, and then beyond the room where the budlings were being kept is a mushroom being that is under the man with no name's control. Oh, but you're too big to fit through the door to get to the other rooms in the palace."

"I can change my size. I can fit. I will turn this wolf creature back to his former self.

<A Doorway Of Mirrors><Return To The Ivory Palace> < By Katrina Mandrake-Johnston >< 36 >
However, I am unable to leave the Ivory Palace. I cannot help this other being you speak of. So who exactly are you, and what do you mean where the budlings *used* to be kept? Where are they now?"

"Oh," Billy said feeling guilty, "I'm Billy. Razzmeara's my grandmother. I'm not from this world."

"Yes, I recognize you now. You are much older since the last time Razzmeara and I saw you through her magic mirror. But, I asked you about the budlings as well," the dragon said with the hint of a threat.

"Yes, well," Billy said hesitating, "The spores this mushroom being shoots out burn the little bug-like creatures there and forces them to collect crystals for the man with no name."

The dragon bent his head down towards Billy and took a whiff. He then snorted and said, "You're infested with one, aren't you? You have a budling attached to you somewhere?"

"On my shoulder," Billy answered nervously, but then added, "But the budling is what protected me from the spores. It's the reason why I was able to get the amulet to rescue you. They are going to use the budlings so they can't be made to collect the crystals anymore. That way, the man with no name can't make any new slaves. There's a chance that the budlings won't behave as their father wishes them to. They say that they want to cooperate, if possible, with the people they attach to instead of forcing them to do what they want. At least as long as they are promised to be well taken care of."

"I see," said the dragon, "and does Razzmeara know that you have released the other budlings?"

"Well, actually no," answered Billy, "but they can't get out of the underground tunnels because of these mushroom barriers that push anyone back that is trying to escape. I thought that if I could save you and Razzmeara was able to come back here, that everything would be all right. If some of the budlings do decide to be bad, I thought that they could be kept away from the room with the father plant and everything would be okay."

"Do you know how to send out the signal to notify Razzmeara that it is safe to return?" asked the dragon.

"No, I don't," said Billy.

"Wait here then," instructed the dragon, "I will contact Razzmeara and change the wolf beast back to normal. Our queen will be able to restore the palace to its rightful state. We had to create this magical labyrinth and then hide it with an illusion on top of that as well, all in an effort to hide the true Ivory Palace from the man with no name."

"Can I check on my mom back in my world? I've been so very worried about her and my dad too. I had to leave them there with my fake sister and a fake me. Than man with no name sent duplicates of us into my world to take our places," explained Billy.

"Yes, of course you can," said the dragon, "but only if you promise to try your best not to get caught. I'm assuming you have the key to the mirror doorways then? You will need to use this large one here to return. As long as the grandfather clock remains where it is now, this gateway should take you to the side yard of your house and not within. Hopefully, it will be safer that way for you."

Billy nodded, and using the mysterious key, entered the shimmering gateway back to his home world.

<< *** >> Next... - Into The Grey Domain <<***>>

A DOORWAY OF MIRRORS

Into The Grey Domain

<A Doorway Of Mirrors><Into The Grey Domain> < By Katrina Mandrake-Johnston >   < 1 >

CHAPTER 1

Billy tumbled out into the yard just outside his house. The mirror gateway he had passed through was nowhere to be seen.

Billy crept up to the living room window and took a quick peek inside. He saw himself and his sister sitting on the couch in front of the T.V. At least he knew where the imposters were now. Maybe he could sneak in somehow and find his mother. They would surely hear him, if he tried to get into the house through a door or even a bottom floor window. Then Billy remembered the big apple tree. Its branches almost reached his mother's bedroom window. She had said that pretty soon they would be able to just reach out and pluck an apple right off the tree from her room.

Billy hurried over to the tree and looked up. It would be a difficult climb and dangerous too. If he slipped and fell, he would be seriously injured.

"Maybe I could get her attention instead?" he thought to himself, *"The branches probably won't be strong enough for me to climb all the way inside the house, even if they do almost touch."*

Billy jumped up and tried to grab hold of the lower branch. It was too high. He tried holding onto the trunk and pressing against it with his shoes in order to wiggle himself up sort of like a squirrel, but that didn't work and he came sliding down.

"If I throw a rock or something, I'll end up breaking the window. That won't be good at all," Billy thought with frustration.

The lacy white curtains were tossed about in the breeze. The window was open.

Billy picked up a small rock and threw it up. It rattled against the side of the house as it came tumbling down again. Was his mother even in her room, Billy wondered. He picked up another rock and did the same. To his relief, his mother stuck her head out the window. Billy waved hello to her, but then she went back inside again. *"Didn't she see me?"* thought Billy, *"Oh no, what if she is a duplicate too?"*

After several minutes, a long rope of bed sheets was lowered out of the window and his mother waved him up with an anxious expression on her face. Billy grabbed hold and began to climb, twisting the rope around his arm and leg for a better grip. When he reached the window, his mother helped him to climb through, and she gathered up the rope and brought it inside as well.

"Billy," she whispered, "I'm so glad you're here. Something awful has happened. They got your aunt. There's a duplicate of Bethany on our side now. I'm being held prisoner here. She takes the imposter children to school and I have no clue as to what they are planning. Worst of all, Billy, is they tricked your father into Jenny's room and they pushed him in through the mirror! No one came out though. If there is no duplicate of him, what does

<A Doorway Of Mirrors><Into The Grey Domain> < By Katrina Mandrake-Johnston >   < 2 >
that mean?!"

"Mom, it's okay. I stopped the man with no name from getting any more crystals. It means he can't make any more new slaves. Dad's okay. He's probably just being held prisoner somewhere. I'm sure he's safe. The man with no name is probably hoping you'll come to the other side to rescue him. I've met Razzmeara. You're the princess over there, right?"

"Yes, that's right. How is she?" she asked him.

"I freed the dragon. Grandma and her people can return to the Ivory Palace now because of it," Billy told her.

"We're going to have to get out of here quickly, Billy," his mother said to him, "If you still have the key, we can get back to the palace from here using the mirror pieces like last time. You're sure it's safe back at the palace?"

Billy nodded and hoped it were true. Once the pieces of the mirror had magically melded into one, Billy held out the key. Then holding tightly onto his mother's hand, they both passed through the gateway.

CHAPTER 2

They emerged into a white corridor, and as Billy looked back to his mother, he was astonished to see that her skin had turned blue just like Razzmeara's.

"Mom! You're blue!" he exclaimed.

"I have a couple feathers as well in my hair," she told him, "but it is only when I am on this side. You already know where I get it from, having met Razzmeara."

"Why don't I have anything weird then?" he asked.

"You might as you get older, Billy. My skin didn't turn blue until I became a teenager, and I actually had more feathers in my hair when I was little than I do now."

"Oh," said Billy, and he wondered if he would soon grow feathers or have blue skin in the future to come.

Billy thought to himself, "*I already have roots on my feet because of the budling, so I guess it wouldn't be so bad if I did. Besides, just like Mom, I'd be normal back home.*"

"Come on, Billy," his mother said with excitement, "I'll show you around. Did you know I used to get to ride the dragon sometimes? Well, just through the halls. There are so many things I'd like to show you, but it will have to wait. We need to find Razzmeara first."

The illusion on the hallways was gone now and they easily made their way to the room where the large mirror and the dragon were. Razzmeara was there speaking with the dragon and Billy's mother hurried over to her. She hugged Razzmeara and then told her what had happened and that Billy's father was now trapped as well on this side. Razzmeara explained all his mother needed to know about the recent activities of the man with no name and what they were doing to try to stop him.

"Mom, Grandma, I saw Jenny. She came up out of one of those metal platforms," Billy told them, "If it weren't for the budling, I would have been killed by the spores."

He went on to tell them about his adventures with Beeshum; how he had used the amulet to turn the dragon back from being stone and how the budling could keep him and Beeshum's people safe from Simpar's spores.

"Then that is where we can get into his grey domain," said Razzmeara, "That will be the one place where it will be unguarded. He will not know about that protection. Billy, you must hurry before he decides to investigate why his crystal supply has run short."

"I could go instead of Billy, Mum," she said to Razzmeara, her voice full of worry.

"No dear, I need your help with another urgent matter," Razzmeara explained, "Billy, you will no doubt need the invisibility potion. Use it wisely, Billy, as you will find that things in the grey domain become drained of energy, including your own stamina and that of the magical potion."

"I will hurry. What should I be looking for once there?" Billy asked.

"We do not know. All that have entered the grey domain have been captured," Razzmeara told him sadly, "With this new entrance opened up to us, however, you will have a much better chance to succeed than any of us."

"I'll try my best," he assured them, and he made his way with Click's help to the lower chamber where Simpar and Beeshum's people were.

CHAPTER 3

He had noticed that a lot of the passageways he had gone through had changed and there were many new doors that had not been there before. Billy ran down the spiraling walkway to the bottom of the chamber and Beeshum greeted him there.

"Billy, so did the amulet work?" Beeshum asked him.

"Yes, and Razzmeara now has control over the palace once more," Billy explained.

"The budlings are working; we aren't affected by the spores anymore," Beeshum told him.

"I'm going into the grey domain to try to stop the man with no name and rescue my family and everyone else's as well," said Billy.

"Do you know how to reverse what he has done to the slaves? Is there a way to get their essence out of the crystals and back into their bodies?" Beeshum asked hopefully.

"I don't know," said Billy sadly, "No one has heard from Squeshna yet. She was the one who was working on a way to do that. I think she might have been caught after all."

"Well, I wish you the best of luck, my friend," said Beeshum with worry, "It will be dangerous. You are very brave and we are all hoping for your success."

Billy stepped up to the platform and the mushroom shuddered to release its spores, but Billy's budling kept him safe. As the reddish cloud billowed about him, Billy stood upon the platform. He began to sink down into it, just as he had done when the man with no name had him sent to the Ivory Palace for

<A Doorway Of Mirrors><Into The Grey Domain> < By Katrina Mandrake-Johnston >   < 4 >
imprisonment.

"*Maybe I should take some of the potion now? I have no idea of where this leads or of whom may be standing by watching,*" Billy suddenly realized, but it was too late and the liquidly metal engulfed him up over his head.

CHAPTER 4

Billy dropped down into a circular room. The walls were made of grey bricks and the floor and ceiling looked almost like grey cement. A single long and narrow corridor led from the room, and Billy could see a light coming from the other end.

He slowly and quietly made his way along it, until he started to come near the end. As soon as he saw what was in the next room, he fumbled around in his pocket, uncorked the bottle, and took a big swallow of potion. Hoping that none of them had seen him, he waited impatiently for the potion to work. So many people were in there, and they were just standing about and swaying slightly. It reminded Billy of a bunch of zombies he had seen once in a horror movie… one his mother had made him turn off before he saw too much of it.

He looked down at his hand and could tell that the potion was working. Soon he would be fully invisible. He fitted the cork back into the vanishing bottle and as he tried to put it back in his pocket by feel alone, the bottle slipped from his fingers.

"*No! How could I have dropped it?!*" Billy screamed at himself in his mind. The tiny bottle broke to pieces with the precious potion running down into a crack in the stone floor.

Billy looked up to see that the attention of each and every slave had been drawn to the sound of the breaking bottle and to his location. The crowd started to push their way toward the narrow corridor.

"*I have to get out of this cramped space or they'll find me for sure!*" Billy thought with panic.

He hurried out into the room. There was more room for him to move about here, but he still had to stay out of their way and keep them from touching him.

Billy jumped away from the flailing arms of one man and ducked under the elbow of a woman. He crawled past the legs of three older boys and stood pressed up against the wall to avoid a little girl.

Finally, he had escaped them, and Billy ran down through the hallway at the other end of the room.

CHAPTER 5

"Click?" Billy whispered taking him out, "Which way should I go? I don't know what to do. What am I looking for here? Are my grandpa and Jenny nearby?"

"Buzz click click," he answered.

"What about my dad?" Billy asked.

"Buzz buzz," said Click.

Around the corner stepped his grandfather, followed by his sister, Jenny. "*Click wasn't kidding when he said they were nearby!*" thought Billy nervously, staring into their familiar faces, "*These are just their bodies. Without their crystals, these two are not really themselves. They are slaves now, and they work for the man with no name. I can't let them find me. They probably heard Click and came to investigate.*"

Billy squeezed past them and continued to run down the passageway. "*If only there were a way to turn them back,*" thought Billy with despair.

<A Doorway Of Mirrors><Into The Grey Domain> < By Katrina Mandrake-Johnston >   < 5 >

CHAPTER 6

Billy went down many different passageways, asking Click at each junction which would be the best way to go. To Billy, all the corridors looked identical; he couldn't tell one from another. Billy felt so very tired. The grey domain was draining his energy. He was quickly becoming visible once more as well, even with the large dose he had taken of the potion. Worst of all was that there wasn't more for him to take now, and he still hadn't found anything that could help.

He felt an electric spark from within his pocket, and Billy pulled out the two marbles. An electric arc jumped out from the marbles and struck the brick wall. An electric blue outline of a door started to come into view. Billy had found a secret door! He put the marbles back in his pocket and pushed open the door. Billy couldn't believe his eyes. The walls, ceiling, and floor of this room were covered entirely by dark purple gems. In the center of the floor, a tall, skinny crystal towered above all the rest, and hovering over the very tip was a tiny blue flame.

"Click?" Billy whispered to him, as he stared in awe of the room, "Does this have something to do with the slaves?" Click answered yes. "If I blow out that flame, will I reverse what has been done with the crystals?" asked Billy with hope.

Amazingly, Click again answered yes.

Delighted, but still wary, Billy walked across the jagged floor, expecting there to be some awful trap. Nothing happened, and he stepped up to the flame. Billy took a deep breath and blew it out.

The room instantly went dark. Billy couldn't believe that the single little flame had been keeping the entire room lit.

"*Did I just save everyone?*" Billy wondered, as he stood there in the dark, "*Could it be that we didn't need to restore each slave separately with each individual crystal?*"

CHAPTER 7

He could still see light coming from the corridor, and Billy hurried out of the room.

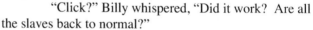

"Click?" Billy whispered, "Did it work? Are all the slaves back to normal?"

"Buzz click click," he replied.

"So I saved them all? I really did it? Can you show me the way back to my sister and grandpa?"

Click said that he could, and he guided Billy back to his family.

"Grandpa! Jenny!" Billy exclaimed with excitement.

"Billy? What are you doing here? I was sure surprised to see Jenny here, but you as well?" said his grandfather.

"Mom's here too with Razzmeara," Billy told him, "But they captured my dad."

"All I remember is that I went into the mirror and then this awful man with an octopus hand grabbed my arm," said Jenny looking nervously around, her eyes wide with fear.

"So you were able to restore those that were made into slaves?" asked his grandfather.

"Yes, well, at least I think I did. I blew out this blue flame in a room full of purple gems," Billy explained.

"Are you two prepared to confront the man with no name? I know where he is. I was captured from behind. I almost had him too. I discovered that it is not only the man. His hand is actually a separate creature. If it is true about this flame, there may be something similar

<A Doorway Of Mirrors><Into The Grey Domain> < By Katrina Mandrake-Johnston >   < 6 >

keeping the old man under the creature's control. We should try to find where it is kept. I'm assuming that he would keep it close. What I saw in the room before I was captured… mind you, this was several years ago now it seems. Anyways, in the room, there was an old oil lamp, a small glass tank with a grey blob of a creature with bright red eyes, and an old grandfather clock much like the one I had. It's from this blob-like creature that the imposters are born. Beside the clock, there is a large mirror which obviously leads back to our home world and to wherever the other clock is. I think that lamp is where we'll find that flame. Come on, I'll show you the way, but please be very careful. You don't know how dangerous this task is."

Billy and Jenny both nodded and hurried after their grandfather down one of the corridors. After what seemed like near twenty twists and turns, they arrived at a large oak door.

CHAPTER 8

"This is it," whispered their grandfather, and he pushed open the heavy door. The three of them rushed in.

The room was how their grandfather had described it. The man with no name said

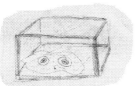

upon their arrival, "Well, I see that you have become more of a nuisance than I had originally thought, young Billy."

"I am here once again," bellowed Billy's grandfather, "Your evil has come to an end!"

The man with no name laughed cruelly and said, "Is that what you think? Attack them now!"

The blob with the large red eyes spit three little grey balls up and out of the tank. Each ball melted, grew in size, and then reformed up into humanoid shape. One resembled Jenny, one looked like Billy, and the other was like their grandfather.

There were now three grey clay-like beings in the room and they ran forward to grab hold of Billy and his family.

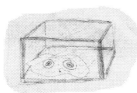

The smaller one grabbed at Jenny's hair and made her cry out as she was then dragged over to the wall. Jenny's arms were next glued to the wall by gooey grey blobs from out of the being's hands. Billy's grandfather was wrestling with the larger being.

The one that was Billy's size was drawing nearer very fast, and Billy knew that he only had a few seconds to do something or all was lost. He dashed forward and knocked the grey being over.

Billy was almost to the lamp, when the being grabbed on tightly to his leg. He was trapped; he couldn't get free.

CHAPTER 9

"Ha! You are all fools!" laughed the man with no name. Billy's grandfather was now stuck to the wall like Jenny.

"Billy," whispered the budling on his shoulder, "I can help. He doesn't know about me yet. What should I do?"

"Try knocking over the tank. It looks like that blob is what controls the duplicates. It might help," suggested Billy.

"Who are you talking to?" snarled the man with no name,

<A Doorway Of Mirrors><Into The Grey Domain> < By Katrina Mandrake-Johnston >   < 7 >
"What are you doing?"

The budling pulled his tendrils out from Billy's shoulder. It stung a little bit, but Billy didn't care. The budling then leapt forward toward the tank.

"No! What's that?!" exclaimed the man with no name. The tank came crashing to the ground and the blob oozed over to the mirror. "No! You can't escape me!" the man shouted at the blob.

The clock began to chime, the mirror rippled, and the blob escaped through the portal. The duplicate beings melted to the floor and vanished. Billy, Jenny, and his grandfather were free.

Billy dashed forward, smashed the glass of the lamp on the table top, and extinguished the blue flame hidden within.

The squid-like mass of a creature dropped from the man's hand down to the floor of the room.

"What? Where... where am I?" stammered the old man.

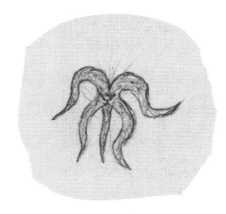

Billy's grandfather grabbed the empty tank. Luckily, the thick glass had not been damaged too badly, and as the purplish-white mass of tentacles wriggled its way over to the rippling mirror while the chimes continued to echo throughout the room, Billy's grandfather kicked the evil creature into the tank with his shoe.

"Come on, everyone, hurry before the chimes end," called out Billy's grandfather, "The creature will be transformed into a harmless object once we get it across to our world."

CHAPTER 10

"Wait," said the man, "I don't understand. What's going on here? Where am I? My name is Steven, now please, who are all of you?"

"Well, Steven," chuckled Billy's grandfather, carefully holding the tank as to not have the thrashing creature within it touch him, "It's a long story. We'll explain once we're safely on the other side."

Billy scooped up the budling and placed him back onto his shoulder. The budling poked in his tendrils once more and Billy came to stand beside the mirror with his sister.

"So did the blob go back to our world, Grandpa?" asked Jenny.

"I don't think so," he answered, "It looks like this clock activates connections to others worlds, as well as our own. We should end up going to wherever our home world is.

<A Doorway Of Mirrors><Into The Grey Domain> < By Katrina Mandrake-Johnston >   < 8 >
Steven here is probably from our world."

They all entered the mirror, and when they exitted back in Jenny's room, all their

grandfather held in his hands was a large grey stone. "I'll keep this former monster safely hidden away in your back garden. Just don't take any rocks with you when you go back through the mirror. We don't want the man with no name coming back with this thing attached to someone else's arm."

"I think I remember something. A nightmare really," said Steven, "I was washing my hands and something fell out of the mirror and onto the counter, as odd as that may sound. I poked at it with my finger and then I don't really remember much after that."

"It looks like the imposters here are gone as well. Most likely all of them sent into our world have vanished like the ones that attacked us. But Grandpa, what about my dad?" asked Billy.

"You and Jenny should go back to Razzmeara and your mother," smiled his grandfather, "Leave me the key, and I'll follow once I've explained to Steven where he's been for the past twenty-five years. It may take awhile."

Everyone went into the next room, and Billy and Jenny went through the mirror leading to the Ivory Palace after the key had activated its portal.

CHAPTER 11

Once back in the Ivory Palace, the two of them ran to the room with the dragon and the large mirror.

"Mum! You're blue!" exclaimed Jenny, "What happened?!"

"We saved everyone and stopped the man with no name. We rescued him even, as it was the creature on his hand all along," explained Billy, "Grandpa's okay. He's coming over here a little later. We couldn't find Dad though or Aunt Bethany."

"That is just fine. We will send in rescue teams to guide the people out and make sure everyone gets back to their proper worlds, including your aunt," Razzmeara told him, "Many are from our world here and I'm sure their families are anxious to be reunited with them. As for your father, Billy, your mother wishes to tell him the truth about this place. After he has seen such mysterious things and since the danger here with the man with no name is gone now, she believes that he is ready."

After some time, Billy's grandfather joined them and they continued to discuss their adventures and how the budling had helped them to defeat the man with no name.

<A Doorway Of Mirrors><Into The Grey Domain> < By Katrina Mandrake-Johnston >   < 9 >

"Do you think Simpar has been turned back to normal?" wondered Billy.

"I am sure he has, as the others have been restored, even the vegetation in what was the grey domain," said Razzmeara with a smile.

"Jenny, Billy, I'll show you to my old room," said their mother.

"I should take a long bath or something. The poor little budling has gone all this time without water," mentioned Billy.

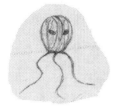

"Thank-you, Billy," said the budling, "So you want me to stay?"

"Of course. I don't mind," replied Billy, "But what about when I go home? I plan to come visit my grandparents a lot here in this world, but I still have to go back and that means you'll have to wait. Things from this world don't come out the same over in mine."

"That's okay, Billy," said the budling, "and besides, with time, because I am connecting with you in such a way, I think I might be able to transfer over to your world with you and remain the same as I am now."

"Yeah, Billy," said Jenny, "I noticed that your shoulder and neck were turning a bit green back home, like you had colored on yourself with a green marker or something. You might want to hide that when you go to school."

CHAPTER 12

Late that evening, after Billy had soaked in a warm bath and Jenny had asked the dragon countless questions and explored a bit of the palace, they were reunited with their father. He had a hard time believing all that had happened, but soon came to accept it.

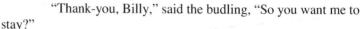

Billy and Jenny said good-bye to their grandparents, and with the key, they followed their mother and father in through the large mirror on their way back home.

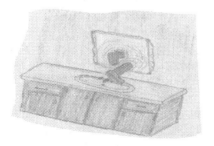

Billy and Jenny had school the next day, as there weren't any imposters to take their place anymore. Their father had to go back to work in the morning, and their mother had a magic mirror to

finish piecing back together. Hopefully, Aunt Bethany would just believe that she had had a very strange dream.

Things were back to normal, at least for now.